INKHEART

MOVIE
NOVELIZATION

P9-DBT-004

INKHEART

Adapted by Jane Mason and Sarah Hines-Stephens
From the screenplay by David Lindsay-Abaire

SCHOLASTIC INC.

New York   Toronto   London   Auckland   Sydney
Mexico City   New Delhi   Hong Kong   Buenos Aires

If you purchased this book without a cover, you should be aware that this book is stolen property. It was reported as "unsold and destroyed" to the publisher, and neither the author nor the publisher has received any payment for this "stripped book."

No part of this publication may be reproduced in whole or in part, or stored in a retrieval system, or transmitted in any form or by any means, electronic, mechanical, photocopying, recording, or otherwise, without written permission of the publisher. For information regarding permission, write to Scholastic Inc., Attention: Permissions Department, 557 Broadway, New York, NY 10012.

ISBN-13: 978-0-545-00709-2
ISBN-10: 0-545-00709-7

© 2008 New Line Productions, Inc. All Rights Reserved. Inkheart™ and all related characters, places, names and other indicia are trademarks of New Line Productions, Inc. All Rights Reserved.

Used under license by Scholastic Inc. All rights reserved. Published by Scholastic Inc. SCHOLASTIC and associated logos are trademarks and/or registered trademarks of Scholastic Inc.

12 11 10 9 8 7 6 5 4 3 2   9 10 11 12/0

Book designed by Rick Demonico
Printed in the U.S.A.
First printing, January 2009

INKHEART

MOVIE NOVELIZATION

CHAPTER ONE

ortimer Folchart ran his fingers across the spines of his beloved books. *Which one to pick?* he wondered. Each book was so special, each with its own story to tell. But he wanted something just right for tonight. His eyes bounced from title to title until he spotted it: *Grimms' Fairy Tales. Perfect*, he thought. He pulled the book out from the shelf and brought it over to his wife Resa, who was sitting warm and cozy by the fireplace. "Here. This should work," Mortimer said. "Let me read to her."

"But, Mo, she's too young," Resa laughed as she looked down at Meggie, their beautiful baby girl. Resa rocked her crib back and forth in an attempt to lull the child to sleep. "Why don't you read to me?" Resa joked with a smile.

Mo smile and opened up the book. "Once upon a time," he began in his soothing, velvety voice.

Resa placed Meggie's bottle on the windowsill and

settled into her seat. She loved hearing Mo read. He had a voice that was pure magic. It was both powerful and soothing, and had the effect of putting Meggie to sleep faster than any lullaby.

He continued the story, pouring out words in his sonorous voice: "There was a dear little girl who was liked by everyone who met her, but especially by her grandmother, who would have given her anything. Once she gave her a little cape of red satin—"

As soon as Mo uttered the word *satin* a glimmer of light shone up from the pages of the book. Mo stopped reading and shot a glance of surprise to Resa.

"What was that?" he asked.

"What was what?" she answered.

"Nothing . . ." he said tentatively. Obviously she hadn't seen what he had seen. Were his eyes playing tricks on him? Was it just the firelight? Mo put it out of his mind and continued the story. "A little cape of red satin," he went on, "that suited her so well that she refused to wear anything instead of it."

Just as Mo finished the sentence, something strange happened. A beautiful red cape drifted silently down from the sky and landed squarely atop the clothesline in Mo's backyard—just out of sight from Mo and Resa's vantage point. The cape wrapped itself around the line, blowing and billowing in the wind, as if it were alive.

"And so she was called Little Red Riding Hood," Mo finished, oblivious to what had just happened in the yard.

Resa reached her arm out where she had placed Meggie's bottle on the windowsill, only to find nothing there. "What did I do with the bottle?" she asked.

"Don't look at me," Mo replied.

"I could have sworn I put it here . . ." Resa's eyebrows furrowed in confusion as she looked from side to side. Where had it gone?

Years later, twelve-year-old Meggie Folchart leaned back in the front seat of Mo's restored Volkswagen camper, admiring the way the snow glistened in the bright, clear day. She and Mo were heading off yet again to some remote European village and some tiny bookdealer's shop to poke through shelves and boxes and stacks of books. The back of the van was packed with crates of old books and rolled-up maps, along with sleeping bags and a portable fridge filled with provisions.

Mo was a bookbinder by trade, and was forever pulling Meggie away from home and school to go on these searches. Though she loved the adventure, Meggie was never quite sure what they were searching for.

"This is the way, right? Up the hill?" Mo looked skeptical. "Hand me that map, would ya?" With his hands on the large steering wheel, Mo squinted up the snowy hill and shook his dark hair out of his eyes.

Meggie unfolded the map, then gazed at her father with concern. He looked tired. They had been to a number of bookdealers already today and Mo had dark circles under his eyes. She wondered if they shouldn't be heading for home.

"You know I have a book report due tomorrow, right?" Meggie asked.

Mo sighed. "This is the last one, I promise."

Meggie bent over the map in her lap, studying it. She had two important jobs on these adventures. The first was chief map reader and navigator. The second, and equally important, was dispenser of chocolate. While her eyes traced the lines of the road, she deftly unwrapped a large bar of Swiss chocolate.

"This is a long hill. Are you sure we didn't miss a turn?" Mortimer asked, still peering anxiously up the road. Then, hearing the crinkling wrapper, he smiled and made a new request. "Give me a piece."

Meggie popped a square of chocolate in her dad's mouth and reassured him they were on the right path. "Positive! It's still up ahead on the right."

Mo savored his treat. His lips curled up in a smile, but his eyes were still full of doubt. "No, it was back there," he insisted, glancing in the rearview mirror.

Meggie resisted the urge to roll her eyes. "You're the driver," she pointed out. "I'm the navigator. Have I ever led you astray before?"

"No," Mo conceded.

"Okay then," Meggie leaned back, satisfied. Mo reached over and snagged the chocolate bar from her slackened grasp. "Hey!" Chocolate stealing was not allowed!

Out of the corner of her eye Meggie saw a small road leading off to the right. "The turn!" she shouted. "Here! Here!"

Mo cranked the wheel and the avocado green camper screeched around the corner.

By the time the chocolate was gone, Mo and Meggie had arrived at their destination. They parked their van on a narrow cobblestone street near a set of steep stairs. Meggie pulled her blue knit beret on over her long pigtails and wrapped her scarf around her neck before climbing out of the car. Together she and her dad climbed the stairs to the center of the village and emerged on another narrow, cobbled street.

"How come every bookstore we go to is a thousand years old?" she teased. "Why can't we ever go to one of those bookstores that sells frappucinos and candy and books that are *new*?"

"What business would a bookbinder like me have in a new bookstore?" Mo replied. "I love old books . . ."

"The marbled endpapers, the leather bindings," Meggie teased in perfect imitation of her father.

Mortimer smiled gamely. His passion for books was no secret, especially not to Meggie. "When you open a book like that, it's like going to the theater. First you see the curtain, then you pull it aside and the show begins."

Meggie grinned. She loved when her father waxed poetic.

The Alpine village they'd arrived in was made up of quaint stone and plaster buildings painted in warm yellow and rose tones. Even in the cold it looked inviting. In the square a stone fountain gurgled, and on the far side, stalls and carts of books spilled out onto the streets.

Mo immediately began to scan the spines, reading titles, looking at each volume with intensity. "My kind of place," he said quietly.

Meggie watched her father run his fingers over the spines. His movements were quick and calculated — he wasn't browsing. He was searching . . . for something. "Maybe you'll find it here, Mo," she said.

"Find what?" Mo asked, distracted.

"The book you're always looking for."

Mo's head jerked up and his fingers stopped moving. "I'm not looking for anything in particular . . ." he said, trying to sound casual. Meggie's observation had clearly made him uncomfortable and he was trying to cover it up.

"Yes, you are," Meggie replied, holding his gaze. She wasn't letting him off the hook. "We never leave a bookstore until you've checked every corner, every shelf. You always come away disappointed. Sometimes," she said more gently, "your eyes are even a little red."

"That's just my allergies. Old books are dusty!" Mo insisted.

Meggie smiled, but was not buying his excuses. She was sure her father was looking for something. She only wished she knew what it was.

CHAPTER TWO

ey look, *Harriet the Spy*." Meggie spotted one of her favorite titles on a cart outside the Alpine Antiquarian Bookshop.

Her father smiled. She had his — and her mother's — love of books. "I'm going inside," he gestured toward the open door of the shop. "Want to come?"

"*The Secret Garden*!" Meggie cried, spotting another favorite.

"You can stay out here, but remember, no reading aloud."

Meggie nodded, mildly annoyed. Her father had given her this same strange warning so many times she didn't bother to look up from the old favorite she was thumbing through to reassure him.

Inside, Mo felt completely at home in the cramped quarters. The shop was stuffed with books, books, and more books, all of them old. The proprietor, a gnomish fellow on a rickety ladder, squinted through his spectacles at his new customer.

"Good afternoon. I'm Mortimer Folchart," Mo introduced himself.

"Ah, the book doctor! You're just in time. Look at this poor patient. Can you save him?" the old man held up a torn volume.

Mo gently took the damaged book and inspected the binding. "I think the prognosis is good," he announced. A bit of glue, a few stitches . . . this book would be like new . . . or even better.

"I've a boxful for you, just like that one," the proprietor said.

Mo didn't flinch. Instead he looked around at the bookshelves appreciatively. "Quite the collection," he said, impressed.

"Small press, limited editions, rare books, mostly." The proprietor paused to watch Mortimer scan the shelves intently. "Are you looking for anything in particular?"

Mo hesitated for a single second. "Uh . . . no, actually." He nodded politely and headed into the maze of bookshelves. Once out of sight Mo began to check the shelves, looking at each title.

As he ran his fingers over the next row of spines, voices began to whisper to him. Some were familiar, some classic, and others new.

"Vronsky! Let us have a drink!"

"My kingdom for a horse!"

"Her name is Heidi . . ."

Mo was not surprised. He had become accustomed to the way books whispered to him. They had been talking to him all his life.

Annoyed that he wasn't finding what he was looking for, Mo let out a small sigh. It was the same story as always. Bending over, he inspected a final dusty bottom shelf.

It was then that he heard it. A woman's voice calling to him from somewhere far away, somewhere deep in the stacks . . .

Out in the square, Meggie had settled on the edge of the fountain with a new adventure book. She knew her father might be a while, and was glad to have everything she needed: a seat, a book, and the perfect snack.

Meggie pulled a chocolate croissant from her coat, unwrapped the crinkly paper and took a bite, brushing a few buttery crumbs from her fingers. While she ate, she watched a girl about her age walking with her parents. They laughed and talked together as they pulled their sleds down the street, and Meggie imagined they were going home to share a warm cup of hot cocoa.

The scene made Meggie want to laugh along with the happy family. It also made her heart ache. Meggie's mother had been gone since Meggie was three years old, and her disappearance had left Meggie with an emptiness that could not be filled. She had never had the chance to sled with her. She could barely remember the last time they laughed together.

Consoling herself with another bite of pastry, Meggie was distracted by a funny chattering noise. She looked down and saw an odd weasel-like animal standing on its hind legs just a few feet away from her. Meggie gave the creature a quizzical look.

The furry brown marten had a body nearly twice as long as its tail, a white face and ears, and dark rings around its eyes that made it look as if it was wearing a small mask. The creature stared longingly at Meggie's croissant with shiny black eyes, and when she did not offer him a piece it chattered insistently.

Meggie tore off a small corner and tossed it to the marten. He gobbled it up quickly and edged closer to Meggie, hoping for more. Smirking, Meggie obliged the little fellow. She tore off another bite and watched it disappear as quickly as the first.

And so it went, bite for bite, until there was just a corner of croissant left. "Come on, boy. Come and get it." Meggie held out the last piece of pastry to coax the animal to climb up beside her.

The marten eyed the girl warily. It was clear that he did not trust her . . . and that he wanted the croissant.

Cautiously, he scurried up. Meggie held out the offering. The marten snatched it and dug in.

Giggling, Meggie reached over to tickle her new friend under the chin. Quick as a wink the marten reared up, hissing and bearing his sharp white teeth. Meggie recoiled and moved away.

"He doesn't like to be tickled."

Meggie turned to see the silhouette of a tall man with shoulder-length hair leaning against a lamppost. The sun was behind him, making it difficult to see his face. Meggie squinted as he walked closer, buttoning his long coat.

"You should be more careful," the man continued. "His name's Gwin. He *looks* charming, but you know what they say about books and covers."

As he approached, the stranger's face came into view, revealing hard eyes and three long scars on one of his cheeks. Meggie recoiled again. There was something ominous about this man.

"Uh yeah, I do. I also know what they say about talking to strangers. Excuse me . . ." Meggie stood and started toward the shop, anxious to find Mo.

"But I'm not a stranger . . . Meggie."

The girl stopped in her tracks but did not turn to face the man. How did he know her name?

"You won't remember me. We only met once, and you were quite small."

*　*　*

"What is that? Coming over the hill?! It's a beast of some kind . . ."

Gooseflesh rose on Mortimer's arm as he followed the whispering voices further into the maze of shelves inside the bookshop. As he scanned the shadows, he dared not believe his own ears. The voices were familiar, but he had been waiting to hear them for so long that he was afraid to entertain even a glimmer of hope.

"My god, it's made of fire!"

Mo's eyes widened and he headed in the direction of the sound. It had been a long time since he had heard from this book, but he could not deny the familiarity of the words. He ducked around a tall shelf and found himself in a dark, forgotten corner.

"Mother! My foot is stuck!" a girl's voice whispered.

Clearing a whole section of books, Mo peered into the darkness of a deep shelf. At once the voices grew louder.

"Brianna, grab your sister!" a woman's voice cried desperately.

Reaching into the depths, Mo felt his fingers close on something flat and covered in dust. A book . . . the book.

"It's The Shadow, we have to run, girls!"

The voices continued as Mo pulled the volume from the shelf and stared down at it. His fingers trembled as he stroked the binding, turned the book over in his hands, and read the worn and dusty cover: *Inkheart*.

Mo's breath came quickly and he flipped through the pages almost desperately. His eyes scanned illustrations of medieval castles, street fairs, and strange creatures, and he paused several times to read a few lines before continuing to thumb through. He was holding *Inkheart* in his hands at last, and still he was afraid to believe it.

A myriad of emotions played on Mo's face. He looked as if he might leap for joy and burst into tears all at once. He paused on an illustration of a marten, then snapped the book shut and strode to the front of the store.

"Find something worth reading?" the proprietor asked, looking up over his glasses.

Grasping the book tightly, Mo replied, "You have no idea."

CHAPTER THREE

riumphant, Mo stepped out of the dark shop into the bright, cold day, but his wide smile vanished when he saw the man speaking to his daughter. In a split second Mo went as white as a page.

"Hello, Silvertongue. I was just talking to your little girl."

Mortimer looked from his daughter to the scar-faced man and back worriedly. Meggie appeared to be fine, just confused. And the man returned Mo's gaze, looking as smug as the marten, who was perched quite comfortably on his shoulder cleaning the crumbs from his face and paws.

"Meggie, go to the van," Mo ordered. Then, seeing the fear in her eyes, he softened his tone. "It's okay. He's . . . an old friend."

"But Dad —" Meggie protested.

"Do *not* argue with me, Meggie! I said get in the

van!" Mo shouted. He saw Meggie freeze. He had never spoken to her like that.

"Let's go for a walk, Silvertongue." The stranger practically smirked. His appearance was creating quite a stir.

Mo gave Meggie a meaningful look. He hoped she understood the gravity of the encounter and the danger she would be in if she did not do as he asked. He had not expected this, nor could he avoid it.

Meggie turned and hurried off without looking back, and Mo drew in his breath, bracing himself. "Okay, Dustfinger," he said.

In the light of the setting sun the two men walked in silence through the maze of small streets that led off the village square.

When they were alone, Dustfinger finally spoke. "I've been looking for you. I've been one step behind you for years, waiting for you to find what you've been searching for."

"Tell me what you want," Mo said. He was anxious to end the conversation and get back to Meggie.

"The same thing you want," Dustfinger replied. "To undo the damage you did nine years ago."

Mo drew in his breath sharply. He had not spoken of that day with anyone, ever.

Stopping, Dustfinger squinted into Mo's face. "And

I have come to warn you. Capricorn knows where you are staying. His men are there now, lying in wait for you and your daughter to come home."

Clutching his bag closer to his chest, Mo tried to quell the panic rising inside of him.

"He has plans for you," Dustfinger continued. "He wants you to read for him."

"Well, he's out of luck," Mo snapped. "I don't read aloud anymore."

"If he finds you, you won't have a choice." Dustfinger rubbed his hands together to warm them.

Mo stared. Dustfinger's fingertips seemed to glow from the inside.

"I can help you, but I won't unless you promise to send me home. I've been here too long." Dustfinger paused and then added, "Send me home, Silvertongue. Read to me."

Mo felt his anger toward Dustfinger dissipate. In truth he felt horrible for the poor man. He was a victim, too. But after that terrible night, he swore never to read aloud again. "I'm sorry I can't help you," Mo shook his head. "That silver tongue of mine is dangerous and uncontrollable, and if I ever use it again it will be for one reason and one reason only."

Dustfinger's mouth tightened, his lips all but disappearing into thin lines. That was not the answer he was looking for. "Then give me the book. If you can't help me, I'll find someone who can." Dustfinger stepped forward menacingly.

Mo stepped back. "I don't *have* the book," he insisted.

"And you never found another one?" Dustfinger asked, suspicious.

"No. I've searched, but . . . I had no idea *how* rare it was. I don't have a copy." Mo looked at his feet. It was only a partial lie. He *had* searched for years. The book *was* very rare. And he *didn't* have a copy . . . until now.

"Why are you clutching your bag so tightly?" Dustfinger asked, taking another step toward Mo.

Looking down Mo saw his whitened knuckles gripping his leather satchel to his chest.

"You haven't let that go since walking out of the shop." Dustfinger paused, letting that observation sink in. "Did you finally find one?"

Only a few doors down, Meggie crouched in a doorway watching the two men speak. She had gone back to the van as her father demanded. But sitting there alone watching the sun set she'd felt confused and annoyed . . . and maybe a little bit scared for her father. She didn't believe the strange man with the scars was an old friend. After a few moments Meggie threw open the van door.

The men had not been easy to find in the small back alleys, but she had located them at last. They looked like they were arguing. They stood close together, her father holding his bag to his chest. The stranger reaching up now and again to pet Gwin. Their voices were intense, but she could not make out the words. Neither man smiled.

Dustfinger knew Mo had found the book — Mo's silence spoke volumes.

"Well that's strange, isn't it? My showing up at the very moment . . ." Dustfinger marveled at the irony of the situation. After nine long years he'd found Silvertongue at the precise moment the man had found the book. "You know there are times in life when the stars simply align."

"Yes, but now is not one of those moments." Mo suddenly whipped around, smashing Dustfinger in the face with his leather case.

Startled, Dustfinger stumbled back into a pile of crates and let out a sharp yelp of pain. The marten on his shoulder shrieked and leaped at Mo — all tiny claws and razor teeth.

Using his case, Mo deflected Gwin, sending the rodent sailing through the air, before turning to flee.

Mo ran as quickly as he could through the labyrinth of snowy side streets. He did not dare slow down or turn around. He could hear footsteps behind him. Dashing around a corner to evade his pursuer, he collided with someone running in the other direction.

"Meggie?"

"What's happening?" Meggie demanded.

"I told you to stay in the van!" Mo shouted, looking over his shoulder. Footsteps echoed on the icy cobblestones, coming closer.

Meggie gave her dad a look. Explanations would have to wait.

Grabbing his daughter's hand, Mo ran as fast as he could toward their van. As soon as it was within sight, Mo charged toward it, diving into the driver's seat. Meggie had never seen her father move so fast. "Hurry, Meggie! Get in. No time to lose!" Meggie couldn't have been more confused, but she did as Mo said and jumped in the van. *SCREECH!* Mo stepped on the gas and off they went, leaving Dustfinger behind them shrouded in a plume of exhaust. Dustfinger stopped, his chest heaving from the exertion of the chase. He shook his head, watching Mo and Meggie grow smaller in the distance. "You fool. I am trying to help you," he cried futilely.

CHAPTER FOUR

o and Meggie drove in stunned silence. Meggie stared straight ahead, shell-shocked. Mo compulsively checked his rearview mirror. He did not know how to explain what had just happened to his daughter. And he was not sure he wanted to.

The sun sank lower and lower. In the dim light inside the van, Meggie reached for Mo's leather case.

"No! Leave it alone!" Mo said. He snatched the case away and tossed it into the back.

"I want to see the book!" Meggie protested. He owed her that after all these years of navigating him to bookdealers, accompanying him on the search.

"You're not allowed to even touch that book, do you understand?" Mo yelled at his daughter for the second time that day.

"No, I don't understand!" Meggie shot back. Her

father was usually very evenhanded with her, and honest. All she wanted to know was what was going on.

"I don't understand at all. What *is* that book? Why does that freaky man with the scars want it? And why did he call you Silvertongue?" Meggie was bursting with questions.

"I can't tell you," Mo said, frustrated.

"You have to tell me," Meggie insisted. He might not want her to get mixed up in all of this, but it was too late for that now.

"No! I have to protect you," Mo insisted. "And your mother," he added under his breath.

"My mother?" Meggie could not believe her ears. Mo almost never spoke of her mother. "What does this have to do with my mother?"

Mo bit his lip and pretended to concentrate on the road wishing he hadn't said anything.

"I'm scared, Mo. What's going on? At least tell me where we are going!" Meggie could not keep the fear from her voice. Her father would not look at her.

"We're going to Italy," he finally said. "You have a great-aunt there. Now please, Meggie — no more questions."

All night Mo drove and his thoughts raced, like the van, through the Italian countryside. It had been in his mind all along to return to his wife's aunt's home when he found the book. Now the time had come.

Driving past the icy blue lake, Mo caught his first glimpse of Elinor's breathtaking mansion. It was as glorious as he remembered, a stately Italian villa on the water. Mortimer and his wife had spent a lot of time here, long ago. It seemed like a fairy tale now . . . something that happened "once upon a time."

A moment later, Meggie and Mo stood together on the front porch. Mo rang the doorbell.

Meggie looked at the plaque mounted in the entry. It read: *Don't even think of wasting my time. Just go away.* "So, she's friendly, this great-aunt of mine?" Meggie asked sarcastically.

"You'll like her . . ." Mo said wryly and pressed the bell again.

Heavy footsteps approached from inside and a voice barked out, "Would you please stop ringing that bloody bell!"

Meggie raised her eyebrows quizzically and looked at Mo as if to say, *I'll like her?*

". . . after a while. She's an acquired taste," Mo added.

And with that the great door opened. Framed inside it was a proper-looking Englishwoman, tall and willowy with sharp eyes, white hair, and a rather grand burgundy jacket. She glared at the intruders who were bold enough to waste her time. But when she looked at Mortimer her glare softened. Realization set in, and her expression turned into a look of amazement. "For the love of Thomas Hardy . . ." she murmured as she ushered her relatives indoors.

An impromptu breakfast of bread, fruit, tea, juice, meats, and cheeses was quickly arranged, and before Meggie could say "Jack Spratt" she was seated at a table on her Great-Aunt Elinor's back patio filling her stomach and enjoying her book with one ear cocked toward the adults' conversation.

"I'm so pleased you've finally found your way back here, Mortimer. Some of my poor books are in desperate need of repair," Elinor announced. Her head was wrapped in a burgundy turban that matched her patterned velvet coat, and her hands were folded at chin height giving Meggie a perfect view of her enormous rings.

"I'll be happy to mend them for you, Elinor," Mortimer obliged.

Not having much of an appetite, Meggie pushed a bite around her plate with a fork.

"Don't play with your food child," her aunt scolded. "Would you prefer some goat's milk yogurt?" She turned back to Mortimer. "She's as thin as a soap bubble. She looks so like her mother, I must say I find it rather upsetting . . . Um, speaking of . . . have you . . . " Elinor was suddenly at a loss for words.

"No, we haven't heard from her," Mortimer sighed.

"Well, no matter. I grew up without a mother and it didn't damage me in any way," Elinor stated.

Meggie wondered if that was supposed to be consolation. From what she had seen so far, Great-Aunt Elinor was a recluse who lived alone in an enormous house with nothing but books.

"I don't think my mother had any interest in children. She dashed off on safari one day and never came back. That's just the sort of thing women in our family seem to do — they disappear off on some adventure. Well, not me. I prefer to stay where I am. Your mother, however, always wanted the real thing."

Meggie gulped. Did Aunt Elinor really think her mother left because she preferred adventure over her own daughter? "My mother wanted *me*," Meggie objected. "And then one day she was *gone*. Without explanation. Is that what you call an adventure?"

"No, I suppose I'd call that abandonment," Elinor mused.

Standing, Meggie ran from the table. She had heard enough.

As Mortimer watched Meggie go, his heart went with her. "Oh, well done, Elinor!" he said, shaking his head.

Elinor sat up a little straighter. Her mouth twitched. "Well, it's the truth."

CHAPTER FIVE

eggie looked across the lake at her aunt's enormous house, scowled, and stuffed her hands deeper into her coat pockets. "Mother did not *abandon* us," she insisted angrily.

"No, she didn't," Mortimer agreed with his hands balled in his own coat pockets.

"Then what really happened to her?" Meggie demanded. She whirled around and looked her father dead in the eye. She was not going to let him evade the question this time.

Mo tried to turn away. For nine years he had been avoiding this moment.

"Mo — look at me. I'm not a child anymore. I'm all grown up!" Meggie said, exasperated.

Gazing at his angry daughter tenderly, Mo sighed. It was true. At twelve, Meggie was no longer a child. Nor was she an adult. She was a girl on the verge of becoming a woman. *"Almost*, Meggie. You're *almost* all grown up," he said gently.

"But I'm big enough to know about the most important thing that's ever happened to me. Don't you think I've figured out why I'm not in regular school like other kids? Why we're always traveling from place to place?" Meggie fumed. "All these years you've been looking for Mom. And that book. I just don't understand how those two things . . ."

"Meggie," Mo tried to interrupt.

"Please, Mo. You have to tell me *something.*" Meggie's anger turned to desperation.

Taking his daughter by the shoulders, Mo turned her to face the sunset and the view of Aunt Elinor's house across the water. "I can tell you this was her favorite spot. And the last place I kissed her," Mo said softly.

Meggie was silent.

Mo bent down, picked up a rock, and sent it skipping across the surface of the water. Meggie studied her dad — the lines of his face, the pain behind his eyes — she could tell just by looking at him that he missed her mom terribly. He ached for her, just like she did. Even talking about her was hard . . . for both of them.

"I write about her sometimes," Meggie confessed.

"You do?" Mo tried to hide the alarm in his voice, but Meggie heard it just the same.

"I make up stories about how she and I —"

"You make up stories?" Mo interrupted, no longer bothering to hide his shock, or his anger. "You know I don't want you to do that . . ."

Meggie knew very well that her father was fearful of the power of words . . . which was exactly why they were soothing to her. "But I have to," she told him. "I feel like the words bring her back to me."

"Yes — the written word — it's a powerful thing. A terribly powerful thing. You have to be careful with it," he said somberly.

Meggie sighed. Her father gave her warning after warning, but no answers. "Do you think we'll ever see her again?" she asked.

Mo paused. "I hope so, Meggie. I hope we do."

Meggie studied her dad's face again, not sure what to believe.

Behind them the sun sank low behind the house.

The next morning after breakfast, Meggie decided to do a bit of exploring. She stealthily made her way down a long hallway to a set of tall double doors. Meggie paused. She knew she shouldn't dare. And yet, she could not resist.

Steeling herself, Meggie took one quick look over her shoulder and reached for the doorknob. She turned it quietly, the door opened, and Meggie slipped inside.

After shutting the door noiselessly behind her,

Meggie stood in the great room with her mouth agape. Never before had she seen so many books in one place — and Meggie had been in many more bookstores than your average twelve-year-old.

Stepping closer to the hexagonal glass case in the center of the room, Meggie leaned in to peer at an old manuscript. The ancient book was open to a page depicting a Middle Eastern pastoral scene. She sucked in her breath. The illustration was gorgeous.

Suddenly a door slammed, and Meggie whirled around to see Aunt Elinor bearing down on her. Color drained form Meggie's face until she was as white as Elinor's dressing gown.

"Step away from the case. Three steps back!" Elinor ordered.

Meggie obeyed while Elinor rushed closer to see if she had done any damage.

"What are you doing in here? This room is not for children. Out! *Out!*" Elinor barked.

Frightened, Meggie complied and headed for the door. "I'm sorry, I-I-I got lost . . . I . . . I was just looking for a book to read."

"Is that a nose print?" Elinor leaned over the glass case, inspecting the small smudge.

Meggie gulped. It *was* a nose print . . .

"Do you have any idea how valuable that manuscript is?" Elinor asked.

"Yes, I do," Meggie answered softly.

Elinor fixed Meggie in a cold stare. She was fed up with the girl's impudence. "Oh, you *know*, do you?"

"It's Persian, isn't it? I can tell from the illumination — the pinks and blues, the gold-patterned background." Meggie spoke with confidence, moving closer to the case and pointing at the details she described. "Maybe from the late twelfth century?" she guessed.

Elinor was stunned into silence by the girl's knowledge, but tried not to show it. "Yes, that's right," she said softly, adding, "what a little know-it-all," under her breath.

Meggie stepped back from the case once more. "It's beautiful," she said appreciatively. She was hoping to soften her bristly aunt, but Elinor was no cupcake.

"As well it should be, I paid a fortune for it," Elinor said, unsmiling. "I adore all things Persian."

"You've been to Persia?" Meggie asked.

"I've been to Persia a hundred times," Elinor answered, waving her arm dramatically. "Along with Paris, St. Petersburg, Middle-earth, distant planets, and Shangri-La. And I've never had to leave this room." She gestured toward the shelves and the worlds held within the books upon them. "Books contain murder and mayhem and love and war!"

Meggie watched, fascinated, as her great-aunt spoke. She clearly shared the family's obsession for the written word. But Meggie thought she saw something else in the old woman's eyes — the flicker of an old wound.

"Books love anyone who opens them," Elinor continued. "They never go away — never. Not even when one treats them rather badly."

Meggie had the feeling her aunt was talking about more than books. She was opening up to her, just a tiny bit. Meggie could see that her aunt had a softer side and she wanted to appeal to it. "Aunt Elinor . . . if I promised not to *touch* anything, could I maybe just . . . sit and *read* in here for a while?"

Elinor stared at Meggie, unsmiling. Without a word she moved to a shelf and took a book from it before gesturing toward the other side of the room. "There's a window seat overlooking the garden. That's where *she'd* always curl up."

"*She?*" Meggie asked.

"Your mother. This book was hers," Elinor said matter-of-factly.

Meggie took the book and clutched it to her chest.

"If I find so much as a bookmark out of place, I'll chain the doors and you'll never see the inside of this room again. *That* I can promise," Aunt Elinor said sternly.

Meggie gulped. Aunt Elinor was going to let her stay!

Without another word the white-haired woman marched to the door and was gone.

Meggie stared at the book in her hand, her mother's book, and read the title: *The Wonderful Wizard of Oz.*

CHAPTER SIX

o rubbed his weary eyes. He was not sure how long he had been at work repairing Elinor's books, but he was bone tired. Last night's reading had taken a lot out of him, but he was determined to do it again . . . and soon.

Taking a fountain pen from his pocket, Mo rubbed it thoughtfully. More than just an ordinary pen, Mo carried the slim object everywhere. It was a talisman of sorts — it helped him think.

Lightning crackled, lighting up Mo's makeshift workbench. Startled by the thunder, Mo dropped the pen and it rolled out of sight.

Outside, the lightning glinted off the wet fur of a small animal — the marten, Gwin — as he scurried through the grass. Stopping, Gwin sniffed the air, then ran quickly to where Dustfinger was staring up at Elinor's manor. The look on Dustfinger's face was a mix of pain, confusion, and determination. He did not like what he was about to do.

Inside, Mo ducked under the table to retrieve his pen. The evening had grown colder, and he shivered as he stooped. If he was going to keep working he would need to build a fire. The thought had barely passed through Mo's mind when there was a bright flash in the room. It did not look like lightning. Mo turned around quickly to see a fire burning brightly in the hearth that had been empty and cold a moment before, and Dustfinger, drenched to the bone, dripping in the corner.

Mo stared, petrified.

"I tried to warn you. I gave you every opportunity to do this the *right* way. But you refused," Dustfinger said. He sounded apologetic and threatening all at once.

Mo backed away, unsure.

"All you had to do was read me back. You could have kept the book. But you ran off, and I had to turn to Capricorn. He promised to help me." Dustfinger's voice was filled with remorse.

Mo shook his head slowly back and forth, not wanting to believe what he was hearing. "What have you done?"

Rain beat ominously against the library window-panes, but inside Meggie was still curled cozily in the cushioned seat, barely aware it had grown dark. She was lost in her book when she heard something and looked up, spooked. Her eyes scanned the room, but saw nothing but books. There was no movement at all.

Still, the whispering continued.

"The Weird sisters, hand in hand, posters of the sea and land . . ."

"I'm Raskolnikov."

"Forehead to forehead I meet thee, Moby-Dick!"

Moby-Dick? With a shiver Meggie realized — it was the books. The books were whispering to her!

Frightened and amazed, Meggie climbed down from her perch and began to walk among the shelves. The voices continued.

"But that is a clue, Watson."

"Yes, I knew before winter. I could smell it coming, but they wouldn't believe me. They feel safe here. Safe! Ha!"

Meggie was dumbfounded. She recognized some of the lines from books she'd read, while other passages were new to her.

Then something else caught her attention. Out of the corner of her eye Meggie saw a dark shape pass by the French doors that led to the garden. Backing away from the glass, she spied another shadowy figure, a man. He was peering at her through the window!

Choking on a scream, Meggie was wondering what to do when the double doors to the library were thrown open and Elinor ran inside. Her eyes were wide with fear.

"There are men outside! They are trying to get in the house!" she cried.

Leaving Dustfinger standing in his workshop, Mo ran as fast as he could toward the sound of shattering glass. He prayed that Meggie was nowhere near it.

Mo's fears were realized when he threw open the door to the library. Men in long black jackets were swarming all over the once-peaceful room, intent on destroying it.

A man with a large red mohawk, a goatee, and black words running from his forehead and across one eye like tire tracks, pulled fistfuls of books from the shelves and tossed them in the air. He was riding one of the library ladders, pushed by another young man with greasy black hair.

Still more men were tossing books through the broken windows, and Mo could see the flickering light of a bonfire burning in the garden below.

In the back of the library a man with a misshapen face, and a nose that looked as though it had been flattened by an enormous thumb, had Meggie and Elinor pinned up against the wall.

"My books, Mortimer!" Elinor shrieked. "Look what they're doing to my books!"

"Mo, look out!" Meggie screamed.

Mo felt a hand on his head, and sharp pain as he was yanked back by his hair and forced to look up into the scowling face of the Black Jackets' leader.

"Basta . . ." Mo said with disgust to the greasy man holding a knife to his throat.

"Hello, Silvertongue. Did you miss me?" Basta leered. His lips curled under his thin, black moustache.

Suddenly the sound of more breaking glass made both men turn. Cockerell, the man with the mohawk, had broken into the hexagonal case and was reaching for Elinor's prized ancient manuscript.

"Illiterates!" Elinor screamed, trapped in her worst nightmare. "Cretins! Those are masterworks you're trampling on! Literary *treasures*! How dare you, you ignorant halfwits?"

In answer to her insults, Cockerell grabbed the Persian manuscript, held it high, and tore it in two.

Elinor's eyes narrowed to slits, she broke free of Flatnose, and charged.

Cockerell watched the old woman's approach with amusement, unsure of what to do next. He could squash her if he wanted to. But while he pondered how to best control her, Elinor landed a solid punch square in Cockerell's face. He staggered back, stunned and confused.

Meggie was watching in horror when the sound of a gun being cocked made everyone stop in their tracks.

Slowly Elinor turned to see Fulvio, a Black Jacket with an eye patch, training his weapon on them.

"Stop it!" Mo commanded, ignoring Basta's iron grip. "Or I swear I'll kill every last one of you. And you know it would only take a few words!"

Fulvio and Cockerell exchanged nervous glances. Elinor and Meggie looked baffled.

Basta calmly flipped his blade over in his hand. His eyes never left Mo, who was trembling with rage. "We won't have to worry about your words if we cut out your tongue," he said. "And if that doesn't work, there's always your daughter's," Basta threatened, taking a step toward Meggie.

It was impossible for Mo to hide the terror on his face at the thought of his daughter being harmed, but before he could do or say anything, Black Jackets swarmed around him, pinning his arms and holding him in place.

"You remember my calling card. One . . . two . . . three . . ." Basta said, looking at Meggie and brandishing his knife.

Breaking free, Mo leaped at Basta, but was blinded by a flash of light.

Dustfinger appeared out of nowhere and stepped in between the two men, his hands inexplicably engulfed in fire. Grabbing Basta with flaming hands, Dustfinger held him against the wall and fixed him in his gaze.

Basta flailed in Dustfinger's fiery grasp. Flames shot up from Dustfinger's fists to lick Basta's petrified face.

"Let go!" Basta pleaded.

"No one gets hurt," Dustfinger said in even tones. "Isn't that what we agreed?"

"Please . . . the fire . . ." Basta was almost too terrified to speak.

"Didn't we agree?" Dustfinger enunciated.

Scared for his life, Basta nodded and was released. He dropped to the floor, panting and patting the two scorched patches on his jacket before rubbing the small good-luck pouch he always wore around his neck. "Evil spirits I repel thee. Evil spirits I repel thee . . ." he chanted.

The flames covering Dustfinger's hands were extinguished as quickly as they had been ignited, but his palms and fingers continued to glow like embers.

In the chaos Meggie dashed past Flatnose and ran into her father's arms. Mo caught her and held tight as the Black Jackets began herding them outside with Elinor.

"All right, get them in the van," Cockerell snarled.

"What? You're taking *them*?" Mo couldn't believe the Black Jackets were kidnapping Elinor and Meggie, too. They had nothing to do with this.

"Capricorn's orders," Flatnose replied.

"After all," Cockerell said with a cruel smile, "we're gonna need a little leverage to make you read."

CHAPTER SEVEN

o looked to Dustfinger. The scowling man with flame-throwing hands was his only hope. "Don't pull my daughter into it," he pleaded, grabbing him by the jacket. "She's just a child!"

Gripping Dustfinger's jacket, Mo felt something hard, square, and familiar under the cloth. Dustfinger tried to pull away, but Mo tore open his coat and saw exactly what he suspected. Dustfinger had stolen his copy of *Inkheart*.

Mo's voice turned to a desperate whisper. "What about my wife? This is my only hope of finding her!"

"And my only hope of ever going home," Dustfinger whispered back, unmoved.

Mo fought the urge to scream at Dustfinger — it wouldn't do them any good for the Black Jackets to know what they were talking about. And he didn't want Meggie to know any more than necessary, either.

"What is this, Mo? When are you going to tell me what's going on?" Meggie demanded. She'd been listening to Mo and Dustfinger's whispered conversation.

Mo knew he should tell Meggie the whole truth, but could not bring himself to do it.

Dustfinger watched the exchange with interest. "Has your father ever read you a bedtime story, Meggie?" he asked meaningfully.

Meggie stared at him, uncomprehending.

"You might want to ask him why that is."

Meggie looked to her father, who was still clutching one side of the book, for clarification. But before Mo could explain, Basta reached over and grabbed the book.

"I'll take that," he boomed, eyeing Dustfinger. "You know Capricorn would want this book for his collection . . . I wonder what he'll do when I tell him you tried to steal it. Now let's go!"

Black Jackets moved in, grabbing Meggie and Elinor and escorting them to the waiting van.

"Don't touch her!" Mo bellowed, lunging at them.

Meggie's eyes widened as one of the Black Jackets raised the butt of his gun. *Bam!* Mo fell to the floor in a heap.

Outside, the bonfire roared, fed by countless pages from Elinor's glorious library. Staring into the flames, Meggie spotted her mother's copy of *The Wonderful Wizard of Oz* and rushed over to retrieve it. But the fire was just too hot.

Suddenly a hand reached into the fire next to her and pulled the book free. Dustfinger. He extinguished the flames and held the book out to Meggie.

Meggie desperately wanted to take the book but could not. Glaring at Dustfinger with pure hatred, she turned away and followed the others to the van.

Disappointed, Dustfinger shoved the book into his jacket and followed.

When Mo came to he was riding in the back of a military van. As the van crept slowly across a stone bridge, Meggie and the others stared in horror at their surroundings. Perched on the side of a steep cliff, the massive village was made up of clusters of dreary stone buildings, many of which were in disrepair. Armed Black Jackets were perched atop roofs and stony outcrops, ready to fire on anyone who dared approach uninvited.

The van slowed to a stop in the town square, and Basta and the other Black Jackets climbed out. A moment later, the back door opened and the prisoners turned to see armed Black Jackets surrounding the van.

"We're here," Flatnose announced.

"How lovely," Elinor replied sarcastically as everyone climbed out of the van. Dustfinger looked at Mo apologetically, but Mo returned his look with a glare. This was his doing.

CHAPTER EIGHT

latnose and Cockerell roughly escorted the new prisoners to the stables — their new home.

As they walked along a row of pens, Meggie tried to ignore the rank smell and the cacophony of noises filling the air — growls, screeches, grunts, and a loud, insistent ticking. "What is this place?" she asked, not sure she wanted to know the answer. Meggie clung tightly to her father as she squinted at the stall slats. She caught glimpses of strange creatures housed in the stables and cringed when her eyes landed on the large beast who would be their cell mate. The creature had the head of a bull and the body of a man. It was unlike anything she'd ever seen.

"Why are we here, Mortimer?" Elinor asked, inching away from the Minotaur. "And where did these *monsters* come from?"

Mo sighed. "Books," he replied resignedly. "They were inside books and that stuttering man read them out. I'd heard of others who could do it, but I've never met one."

Meggie stared at her father and tried to wrap her mind around what he was saying. "Read them out? What do you mean?"

"Be clear, and make it quick, Mortimer," Elinor instructed impatiently. "Or I swear I'll disinherit you."

Mo closed his eyes for a second, gathering strength. It was so painful to talk about that night . . . but he couldn't keep it in any longer.

"You were away, Elinor, at a book fair. We were house-sitting for you. Me, Meggie . . . and Resa. We had brought a couple of books along, and one of them was *Inkheart*."

He could picture it so clearly in his mind's eye. Little Meggie flipped through her dragon picture book near the fire while her mother sketched with a fountain pen — the one Mo still carried with him.

"I was reading *Inkheart* aloud. It was a good read — adventure, magic, a mob of villains . . . and The Shadow, a creature so terrifying . . ."

Mo stopped himself from describing the beastly thing any further. "I read several chapters and nothing happened. But then there was a gust of wind, and the lights flickered. When I looked up, I saw a tall figure before me, looking weak and disoriented. I recognized him as Capricorn from the description in the book."

Mo paused for a moment, almost afraid to go on. But it didn't matter — what was done was done.

"Staggering back, I bumped into Basta just as Dustfinger appeared out of nowhere." Mo remembered the look of sheer terror in Dustfinger's eyes.

"When I turned back to my family, Resa was gone . . . her wedding ring was spinning on the floor as if it had fallen off the table. The ring, and her fountain pen, were all that remained behind."

Mo looked at Meggie in the dim light of the stable, his eyes full of tears. "My voice brought them out," he said sadly.

"Your voice brought them out. Of the book," Elinor repeated, not believing.

Mo turned to Meggie. "And your mother went in. That's how it works."

"How it works?" Meggie practically screamed. This was too, too much.

Mo reached into his pocket and pulled out his fountain pen — Resa's fountain pen — and held it lovingly.

"My God, Mortimer," said Elinor, slowly beginning to grasp the truth of the situation. "All this time I thought the worst of Resa. Why didn't you tell us?" Elinor wondered.

"Would you have believed me?" Mortimer asked desperately.

The Minotaur stepped out of the shadows and sniffed Elinor's hair. "Would you have believed that?"

"You want to read Mom back out," Maggie blurted, suddenly understanding. "That's why you've searched for *Inkheart* all these years."

Mo nodded sadly. "And just when I finally find the book, Dustfinger steals it from me . . . not that I blame him."

"Not that you blame him?!" Elinor screeched. "He led those villains to my house. To us!"

"He needs the book, too," Mo said reasonably. "He's trying to get home any way he can. I've always hoped Resa's doing the same thing."

"If she's alive, you mean," Meggie said sadly. She had so many emotions crashing around inside of her — confusion, joy, sadness, fear . . . .

"How do we know if she's really trapped in that book? Who's to say she even got there? And how could she survive for nine years?" Her eyes welled with tears as she gazed at the Minotaur. "If the monsters are any-thing like this one . . . or worse . . ." Meggie felt tears threatening to spill down her cheeks as a sob escaped her throat. "How do we know where she is? Or if she's even alive?"

Mo's heart ached for his only daughter. They didn't know, of course. They simply had to believe. Sliding closer, he wrapped his arms around her, cradling her head on his shoulder while she wept.

CHAPTER NINE

ut in the village, Basta and Fulvio escorted Mo, Meggie, and Elinor toward the castle. As the blackened, crumbling tower came into view, Mo nearly fell back.

"It looks just like the picture in the book," Meggie murmured fearfully.

"What a perfectly hideous edifice. It's an architectural cacophony. The man clearly has no taste," Elinor decried.

Moments later, the prisoners were led down a long hall painted with scenes from *Inkheart*. Beautiful pastoral scenes gave way to medieval castles and bloody battles.

Mo reached for his daughter's hand. "Just pretend we're in a book," he advised in a whisper. "Kids always escape in books."

"No, they don't," Meggie retorted. "Remember *The*

Little Match Girl? They found her in an alley frozen to death."

Mo tried to ignore the sinking feeling in his stomach as the murals became even more gruesome, filled with images of a city leveled by an ungodly monster made of fire and ash.

"The Shadow," Mo murmured under his breath as they approached a giant room lit by a thousand candles. Black Jackets stood guard against the walls, and a dour-looking, elderly maid dressed all in black, stood near the roaring fire next to Capricorn himself.

"Come in, we saved you the good seats," Capricorn greeted them with a sinister grin.

Mo stared at the man standing in front of him. He looked nothing like the character he had read out of *Inkheart* nine years before.

"You got old," Capricorn said derisively.

"You got a castle," Mo replied.

"Indeed, I did. And one in a lovely, secluded part of the country, far from prying eyes. I've adjusted quite well to your world, haven't I?" He smiled, then turned his attention to Meggie.

"This scrawny little thing must be your daughter. So much life to live . . ." he eyed Elinor derisively. "You, however, are a noisy old bag. You make a racket without even opening your mouth."

Elinor stepped forward, unafraid. She had a bone to

pick with this hooligan. "Now look here, you barbaric piece of pulp fiction. Your malice matches your stupidity — I don't know what things are like in that wretched third-rate novel of yours, but where I come from one does not ravage libraries!"

Capricorn regarded her for a mere half a moment before waving his hand. An instant later two Black Jackets had gagged her and were dragging her to a corner and tying her to a chair.

"Mo!" Meggie shouted. Her father had to do something!

"I have no patience for old women with big mouths," Capricorn stated, turning to his elderly maid. "Do I, Mortola?"

Mortola smiled proudly, enthralled by his cruelty.

"I'd like to introduce you to Darius, my reader," Capricorn went on, gesturing to a timid-looking man who sported a bowler hat and round spectacles. Darius was sitting on a crate, and in his hands he held a frayed copy of *Greek Myths*. "I think he's happiest of all that you're here. Darius, let's show our guests what I've been up against."

He tossed *Grimms' Fairy Tales* across the hearth and it landed at Darius's feet. A nervous wreck, Darius stared at him in disbelief.

"B-b-but you said I wouldn't have t-t-to read once he got here."

"Yes, well, I lied when I said that. Now open the book."

Darius did as he was told, and soon his meek voice echoed softly in the large chamber. "Rapunzel had magnificent long hair, fine as spun gold, and when she heard . . ."

Suddenly a frightened young woman with ridiculously long hair landed on the floor and ran across the hall in search of a handsome prince . . . only to be caught by a pair of laughing Black Jackets.

"You see? Look at the writing. She's only half out of the book," Capricorn sneered, pointing at the black text printed on the frightened girl's skin. "Take her to the kitchens. *Another* maid. And give her a haircut!"

"I won't read aloud, if that's what you're intending," Mo insisted, watching the poor girl being dragged off. He nodded toward his daughter and his aunt. "Not while they're in the room."

"Bring the girl up," Capricorn ordered.

A Black Jacket moved toward Meggie, but Mo bashed him in the mouth. All around him, other Black Jackets cocked their guns. Mo froze in place, terrified.

"Here's how this is going to work," Capricorn stated. "You do whatever I say, or I'll kill the old lady and lock your daughter in the dungeon for all eternity." He smiled cruelly, then grabbed a book from Darius's basket and tossed it to Mo. "Let's get started, shall we?"

Mo looked helplessly at the book in his hands — *One Thousand and One Arabian Nights.*

"It's a good one," Capricorn assured him greedily. "Filled with riches."

Mo shot Capricorn a look. "I'm reading out treasure?"

"For now. *Someone* has to pay for all the repairs around here. The locals have been bled dry."

Mo looked over at his daughter and aunt, his heart filled with fear. What if they disappeared into the book? Then again, if he didn't read, they'd disappear anyway.

"I can't control what comes and goes," Mo warned Capricorn. "There's no telling what might happen."

"Well, this should be fun then," Capricorn sneered.

Dustfinger watched anxiously as Mo cracked open the book and began to read. "Kasim gazed upon the treasures within the cave. Mounds of gold and silver were heaped from floor to ceiling. Piles of silks, and sacks of jewels," his deep voice resonated against the stone walls, nearly hypnotizing everyone in the room. Meggie, in particular, was riveted.

"Kasim gathered all the treasures he could carry, only to find the door of the cave sealed shut. And by the will of Allah, he had forgotten the password. Kasim named every grain he could think of — 'Open Barley! Open Buckwheat! Open Millet!' but the door did not budge. And then came the sound of approaching hooves."

Fulvio listened intently as beads of sweat gathered on his brow. He nudged Basta and pointed to the floor. "Look . . . sand."

As Mo read on, wind swept through the grand hall, blowing sand and dust. Scorching sand poured through the window.

"Kasim ran to hide, but tripped, sending coins spilling in every direction. Then came the muffled cry of 'Open Sesame,' and the cave opened, revealing a swarm of bandits."

As Mo continued to read, a magical waterfall of coins spilled down from the sky and onto the floor of Capricorn's palace. Treasure rained down . . . gold coins, gems, and pearls. Capricorn shoved his hand into a sack of gold, running his fingers through the coins. "See how it's done?" he sneered at Darius.

Mo stepped away from the mounting riches, shocked. His reading aloud never had this kind of impact before, and he wasn't sure how to respond.

Suddenly a figure darted out of the shadows, looking like a petrified rabbit. The boy wore a dirty vest, baggie genie pants, a turban, and clearly had no idea where he was. Several Black Jackets leaped into action, chasing him around the room. After several hectic minutes, they managed to trap the terrified boy in a corner.

"Look! What did I tell you!" Mo half shouted.

"But if he came *out*, who went *in*?" Meggie whispered in alarm.

In the world of *One Thousand and One Arabian Nights*, Fulvio stared at his desert surroundings . . . and forty of the meanest snaggletoothed thieves he'd ever seen.

"Put the boy in the stables," Capricorn ordered. "We can feed him to the malformed Minotaur."

Meggie, her eyes wide with fear, turned to her father. But Mo was helpless.

"It's my turn now, like you promised," Dustfinger suddenly blurted, stepping forward.

"Your turn?" Capricorn sounded surprised. "Oh, you mean *this*?" he held up a copy of *Inkheart*. "Incredibly rare, this book." He settled his gaze on Mo. "I'm surprised you found one. We've been tracking them down for years, in shabby lending libraries and secondhand bookshops. These local boys interning with us are very good at digging things up."

"I can't send anyone back," Mo insisted. "I don't know *how*."

"Send us back? Why would we ever want to go back when your world is so much more accommodating? With your telephones and guns and —" he turned to Basta. "What's that sticky stuff called?"

"Duct tape."

"Yes! Duct tape! I love duct tape!" Capricorn crowed. Then his eyes narrowed. "Besides, what was I in *Inkheart*? A fire-bug. Living in the woods with all those filthy creatures." He shuddered ever so slightly at the memory. "But look at me now. I have a castle!"

Standing at Capricorn's side. Mortola surveyed the great hall proudly.

"No, I like it better here," Capricorn concluded. "I'll never go back. None of us will. And to make sure of that, I'm going to do what I always do when someone digs up a copy of this tedious book . . ." He quickly approached the raging fire in the hearth.

Dustfinger's eyes flashed with panic. "You promised I'd be sent back!" he shouted.

"Yes, I know. I *lied* when I said that. I'm a liar. I lie all the time. Lie, lie, lie!" He turned back to Mo. "After all these years you'd think he would've figured it out by now," he said, casually tossing the book into the fire.

"Noooo!" Mo and Dustfinger screamed in unison. Dustfinger raced forward and plunged his hands into the flames after the book. His face contorted with pain, he let out an agonizing scream and dropped the

Meggie

Farid

Elinor

Dustfinger

Resa

Basta

Mortola

Flatnose

Silvertongue

flaming book at his feet. He stared down at his damaged hands and the flaming pages below.

"Must you do that *every* time?" Capricorn asked tiredly. "It's pathetic, honestly."

Basta and several Black Jackets laughed while Dustfinger stared at the now unrecognizable copy of *Inkheart* lying at his feet. Capricorn strode over, picked up the charred book, and tossed it back into the flames.

"Go and have your burns tended to — otherwise I'll have to cancel our weekly juggle night," Capricorn said lightly before turning to a handful of Black Jackets. "Lock the others up. We'll continue where we left off tomorrow."

Dustfinger looked helplessly at Mo, who returned his gaze. They were trapped together in a horrible nightmare.

Chapter Ten

n the stables, the prisoners huddled together in their filthy pen.

"It's just a dream. It's just a dream. It's just a dream." The long-haired boy from *One Thousand and One Arabian Nights* chanted, hugging his knees to his chest tightly.

Maggie felt awful for the boy. "Are you all right?" she asked gently. "What's your name?"

"My name is Farid," the boy answered in a whisper.

"Are you one of the forty thieves?"

Farid looked up sharply, his face a fury. "Stop talking to me! Don't you know it's unlucky to talk to someone in a dream, you stupid girl! If you talk in a dream, you never find your way back."

"Stupid?!" Meggie shot back angrily. "You're the one who thinks he's in a dream! I was just trying to be nice!"

"He must have a plan of some kind," Mo interrupted the squabbling teenagers. "Capricorn spends every page of *Inkheart* spreading his villainy. If he intends to stay here I can guarantee he'll do what he's always done."

Elinor looked up, still rubbing her wrists where they'd been tied. "And what is it he's always done?"

All at once Mo realized he'd already said too much.

In the castle kitchen, a beautiful maid with short blond hair shoved the tip of a knife blade into a large padlock — the one holding the chain around her ankle — and turned it carefully. Her heart pounded with the hope of freedom, but the blade snapped in two. Again.

While she cursed the heavy chain that tied her to the kitchen table, footsteps echoed in the hall. The maid quickly shoved the broken knife up the sleeve of her scarlet dress and began to scrub the kitchen floor on her hands and knees.

A moment later a pair of men's boots stopped right next to her. She looked up to see Dustfinger, with Gwin on his shoulder, standing over her. He held his charred hands up sheepishly.

"I've hurt myself again," he said.

The maid's face filled with sadness and sympathy, and she began gesturing to Dustfinger reproachfully.

"Don't scold, Resa," Dustfinger said as she motioned for him to sit near the hearth while she fetched a bowl of ice.

Dustfinger stared into the flames dubiously. "Fire is so unpredictable in this world," he muttered. "In Inkworld, I never burned my hands. Here, it is a trickster."

Resa held out a bowl of ice. But as she gently put Dustfinger's hands into it, the broken blade slipped out of her sleeve.

"You've tried to escape again," Dustfinger said understandingly.

Resa shrugged silently. The printing on one side of her face looked elegant, like a tattoo.

"It looks like neither one of us is going anywhere. Only hours ago I held *Inkheart* in my hands."

Resa brightened for an instant, but then Dustfinger went on. "It's ashes now, thanks to Capricorn. It was my last chance to get home — and now I'll never see my . . ."

He trailed off, his eyes full of sadness. "It's over for me. I'll never see my home or my family again. But you . . . you still have hope." He turned to face her. "I saw Darius read you out of Inkworld. He left your voice behind in the book. If you could talk, would you tell me your story?"

Resa looked away, unable to answer.

"You don't trust me. It's because of how I'm written, isn't it? I'm supposed to be weak and deceitful but that's not the real me. I'm not just my character, you know."

Resa smiled sadly, wanting to believe him but not certain that she could. So instead she put a pillow behind Dustfinger's head and encouraged him to rest.

Thankful for the opportunity to lie down, Dustfinger quickly dozed off. As soon as he closed his eyes, he was fast asleep and transported somewhere far, far away. He found himself in a bustling town center, with all eyes on him as he began to perform for the crowd. As he nimbly juggled balls of fire, he heard the voice of a child. "Daddy, come home!" the child called. "Come back to us," a woman's voice echoed. Dustfinger whirled around to see his wife and child standing side-by-side behind him. His eyes filled with tears. He was finally home!

In the light of early morning, Dustfinger sleepily opened his eyes. He awoke next to the hearth to see Resa working nearby. He hadn't returned to Inkworld; it was all just a dream. He looked down at his hands and saw that they were freshly bandaged. Resa had tended his wounds while he slept.

"And what can I do for you in return?" he asked her.

Resa pulled on her shackles meaningfully.

"A key? I wish," he eyed her, wanting to know more about her, about her dreams. "And if I found you one, where would you go? Tell me, what makes your eyes so sad?"

Resa paused, then reached into her pocket and pulled out a crumpled, faded drawing of a man and a little girl.

Dustfinger stared, unbelieving. He knew them! "Your husband? Your daughter?"

Resa nodded, her eyes welling with tears.

"You went in when I came out!" he murmured.

Resa searched his face, silently pleading for more information.

"What if I told you that what you've been wishing for is very, very close by?"

A silent sob escaped Resa's throat, but she dared not believe. Could Dustfinger be telling the truth?

"I'll get you out of these chains. At least one of us can still find the way home." He summoned Gwin to his shoulder and they rushed out, leaving Resa yanking on her chains.

A few minutes later Dustfinger carefully cracked the door to Mortola's room. Luckily the old maid was snoozing peacefully in an easy chair, surrounded by framed photos and newspaper clippings of Capricorn's exploits.

"See that key?" Dustfinger whispered to his pet. "Steal it and bring it to my friend in the kitchen."

Gwin scurried into the room and climbed up the side of the easy chair, onto Mortola's shoulder. Outside the door, Dustfinger gave Gwin an encouraging nod.

Gwin stared at the key ring, which was tucked in Mortola's shirt. Stretching his torso, he reached in . . . just as the old maid stirred in her sleep. When she had resettled, Gwin pulled the key ring the rest of the way out of her black bodice.

"Ahhhhh!" Mortola sprang awake and screamed, reaching for her shotgun just as Gwin escaped out the door after his master. "I'll make a fur collar out of you!"

Mortola fired several shots, but Dustfinger was already gone and Gwin had hidden himself under a bush, clutching the ring of keys. As soon as the coast was clear he dashed to the kitchen and dropped the ring of keys on the table.

Grateful, Resa tossed him a crust of bread and then set to work finding the right key.

In the stables, a worked-up Mo was pacing and talking, half to himself. "Something was different when I read. I was never so in control of it! I know I can get Resa out of the book, and maybe send Capricorn back in. We just have to get another copy."

"It took you nine years to find the one you did!" Elinor said dejectedly. She wasn't one to be deterred by adversity, but had never been captured by an evil character from a work of fiction before!

"I bet the author has a copy," Meggie said thoughtfully. "If he's alive, I bet *he'd* have one. You know all kinds of people in the book business. Someone has to know where he lives . . . ."

Mo and Elinor stared at Meggie, dumbstruck. Why didn't they think of that before?

"Oh, drat," Elinor said, suddenly realizing what this meant. "We're going to try to escape, aren't we?"

"It's either that or get fed to one of those horrible creatures next door," Meggie pointed out.

"Someone has to stop him," Mo insisted. "You don't know what Capricorn is capable of!"

Just outside the pen, Dustfinger listened intently. He'd come to tell Mo the news about Resa, but now realized that there was still a chance he could get home — if only they could get their hands on a copy of the book. In an instant he had made his decision: Resa could wait.

Working quickly, Dustfinger picked the lock on the pen door. Silently pulling the door closed behind him, he noted the angry looks on the faces before him.

"Before you say anything, just know that I'm here to save your necks."

"After putting them on the chopping blocks, you mean?" Elinor practically hissed. She was still furious about her library.

Dustfinger ignored her and turned to Mo. "You want your wife back as much as I want to go home. If you think there's a copy of *Inkheart* out there, let's find it together."

"And how will we escape?" Mo asked.

Dustfinger reached into his pocket and pulled out the scorched copy of *The Wonderful Wizard of Oz* he had rescued from Elinor's library. As he tossed the book to Mo, Mo's eyes lit up. A tornado should do it . . . .

A few minutes later a funnel of dust and wind began to spiral dangerously in Capricorn's village. A newly freed Resa stared at the sky from her basement hiding place anxiously. Black Jackets ran for cover. Darius dashed from pen to pen to try and calm the fretful beasts.

In the prisoners' pen, Mo closed the book with a satisfying snap. Wind howled around them, shaking the stable walls. Meggie rushed into her father's arms, and Gwin scurried into Dustfinger's pack.

Outside, the cyclone sucked up trees and small buildings. From her hiding spot Resa watched, hoping against hope that this wasn't the end. And then she spotted several figures making their way along the outside of the stable walls. Dustfinger was there, and a boy she didn't recognize. And Elinor! And Mo! And could that possibly be Meggie . . . her own darling Meggie?! Overcome by emotion, Resa longed to call out, but had no voice. She longed to go after them, but there was a tornado in her way.

She was completely powerless. Wiping tears from her face, she watched in agony as her family escaped without her.

CHAPTER ELEVEN

ighting against the howling wind, Mo and his crew made their way to the van they were kidnapped in and climbed inside. Moments later, with Mo behind the wheel, the van was racing out of the village, Mo doing his best to avoid the flying branches and fence posts swept up by the tornado. And then, as the storm cleared, a small Kansas-esque farmhouse fell from the sky and landed with a resounding *THUD!*

Mo eyed Dorothy's house but kept driving. He drove all day and into the night. As the van made its way up a twisting mountain road, a pair of suspicious-looking Black Jacket cars followed at a distance, expertly maneuvering around corners.

"Still think you're dreaming?" Meggie asked Farid, as she clutched the side of the wildly swerving van.

"What else could it be! We're flying! Or is it the

night flying past us?" Farid asked, staring into the darkness with wide eyes.

Mo drove throughout the night. By morning everyone was exhausted, but they had arrived at Alassio, a small and very beautiful village on the Italian coast.

"This is the town," Elinor reported, as the group sat in the piazza, munching freshly baked croissants she'd purchased from a nearby bakery. Upon their arrival in Alassio, Elinor had done a bit of investigating and returned with breakfast, clothes for Farid, and some important information. "The woman in the fish store says he lives in the apartment with the terrace overlooking the town square."

"I'm not going up there," Dustfinger announced.

"But you have to," Mo insisted. "He won't believe me otherwise."

"You can be pretty persuasive," Dustfinger replied. "You talked us out of our books, after all."

"What's the matter with you?" Mo asked. "The book is within your grasp and suddenly you're . . . ."

"He's afraid," Meggie blurted, suddenly realizing. She gazed at Dustfinger. "You've never actually read *Inkheart*, have you?"

"What's there to read? I've lived most of it. Except for the end, and *that* I have no interest in."

"Why not?"

"You don't know the end of your story, do you? And

I suspect you wouldn't *want* to know it. It'd be like flipping to the last page of a mystery story. Where's the fun in that?"

"Well, I think I know the end to my story," Elinor interrupted. "Mo, Meggie, I'm going home. This brutish world of mud and flies . . . well, I'm sorry, I prefer a story that has the good sense to stay on the page where it belongs. I must rescue my poor, desecrated books and mend them and put them in order. I need the quiet world of my library." She thrust some money at Mo, then awkwardly shook his hand and kissed Meggie. A minute later she was gone.

Mo rang the doorbell of the author's apartment and stood nervously next to his daughter waiting for a response. When the door finally opened he was somewhat surprised to see a mild-looking older man wearing an apron.

"*Signor* Fenoglio?" Mo asked.

"Yes?" the gentleman replied.

"Sir, my name is Mortimer Folchart, and we were hoping to . . . ."

"Yes, yes, just give me something to write with, but be quick about it. I have a cake in the oven," the author replied. He wiped his hands on his apron, clearly expecting them to follow his instructions.

Confused, Mo and Meggie just stood there.

"Well, don't stand there like you've been taxidermied! If you want an autograph, give me a pen!"

"But . . . we don't want an autograph," Meggie explained.

"You don't want an autograph? Then why in the name of Chaucer's beard did you ring my bell?"

Mo swallowed hard. This wasn't how he'd hope things would start, and he wasn't quite sure how to explain. "You're never going to believe this," he began, smiling half-heartedly.

Back in the piazza, Farid stood in front of a shop dressed in high-tops, new jeans, and a plaid shirt, staring at his reflection. Behind him, Dustfinger watched the street entertainers juggle, dance, walk on stilts, and perform magic tricks. As he watched, memories of his own performances come flooding back . . . along with visions of his wife and two lovely daughters.

Before he knew what he was doing, Dustfinger had removed his shirt and was on his feet before the crowd. He took a swig from the blue bottle he kept in his pack, then snapped his fingers, creating a flame in his hand. Holding the flame up, he sprayed it with the liquid in his mouth. An impressively long stream of fire erupted from his mouth while the crowd oohed and aahed.

Next, Dustfinger made a circle, the flames cutting through the air like a flame thrower. When he finished, he spit on the ground.

"That was amazing!" Farid crowed.

Dustfinger shook his head. "That was nothing. You should see me in my world."

"What was that at the end?"

"It's called Dragon's Breath."

"Teach it to me!" Farid begged.

Dustfinger chuckled at the boy's eagerness as the crowd dispersed.

Meanwhile, Meggie and Mo were walking with Fenoglio through the piazza.

"It's a good story, I'll give you that," Fenoglio mused. "*Silvertongues*. Great concept — wish I'd thought of it! But it's too absurd to be taken seriously. I know my characters are so lifelike that they seem to jump off the page, but it's simply not possible that . . . ."

They rounded a corner, and Fenoglio spotted Dustfinger immediately. The writer stopped dead in his tracks.

"Exactly as I imagined him. This must be what it feels like to give birth." Fenoglio mused as he began to force his way through the crowd.

"Hey! Where are you going?!" Mo called. "He doesn't want to meet you!"

"Of course he does," Fenoglio waved him off. "I'm practically a father to him."

Mo dashed after the writer. "Look, I know the idea of meeting your characters must be very exciting for you, but the whole point of coming here was for you to help us send them back into the book."

Fenoglio stopped, clearly irritated, and pulled a notebook and pen out of his pocket. He began to scribble furiously.

"Your father has given me an idea for a character," he said to Meggie. "A master-thief, who steals things the way a blue jay swipes shiny objects off of window sills."

"I am not stealing your characters!"

"You snatched them out of my book!" Fenoglio replied hotly. "You're trying to keep them from me! That, my friend, is pure thievery!"

"I'm just trying to get my wife back!" Mo practically screamed.

Fenoglio tucked his notebook back into his pocket and marched off, with Mo on his heels. Meggie watched them go, not sure what to do. She had a feeling this would not end well.

Dustfinger was packing up in the center of the piazza when he turned to see an old man gawking at him like an awestruck teenager.

"Dustfinger . . . ." the man said breathlessly.

Dustfinger looked to Farid, confused. Who was this weirdo?

"I tried to stop him, but. . . ." Mo explained, rushing up to them.

"So very nice to meet you! The scars are perfect, as hideous as I imagined!" the old man said, with obvious delight.

Dustfinger stared at the man, overwhelmed by a plethora of feelings.

"I told you, Fenoglio. He's afraid," Mo said quietly.

"Of what? Not of me, I hope," Fenoglio babbled.

"Of the end of the book."

"What do you mean?" Fenoglio looked completely baffled. "Because he dies?"

Mo watched Dustfinger's face crumple, then lowered his head in defeat. "No, because he didn't want to know what happens."

Fenoglio paled slightly. "Oh. Right. Sorry."

"He dies in the end?" Meggie asked, aghast.

Mo turned. He hadn't known she was there!

"I had to make the story *exciting*. That's my job! And they can't *all* have happy endings. *Life* doesn't always, after all."

Dustfinger stepped forward, grabbing Fenoglio. "How? How does it happen?" he begged.

"You're killed by one of Capricorn's men. While trying to save Gwin. It's a very touching scene. . . . I cried when I wrote it."

"How nice, I have something to look forward to," Dustfinger said, his voice dripping sarcasm.

"Look forward to? Heavens no, you can't go back. They'll kill you for sure. You'll stay here instead. I have a guest room."

Dustfinger was shaking now. "You think I care what you wrote? You are not my god. I am not a *character* and you do not control my fate! If you did I wouldn't have wound up *here*." He stopped for a moment, pulling himself together. "I'm going back. Do you have a copy of the book or not?"

Fenoglio held Dustfinger's gaze, impressed with his creation.

Up in Fenoglio's attic, the search for *Inkheart* was all encompassing. Fenoglio ripped open box after box of books, looking for a copy.

"The problem is, it's been out of print for decades. Plus the original run was quite small. And then there was the fire at the warehouse, and eventually the publisher went out of business," Fenoglio rambled.

"I did hold onto a few copies, but then I loaned them to a book exhibition in Genoa a few years ago, and they were stolen. I suppose Capricorn was behind the theft, but at the time I simply assumed it was bad luck."

Before long a mountain of boxes had piled up in one corner, but *Inkheart* had not been unearthed. Until finally . . .

"Oh, here we are, then!" Fenoglio held up two stacks of old, unbound pages.

"What is that?" Dustfinger asked incredulously.

"It's the book, the original manuscript. Look at that — typewritten! Can you imagine?"

Dustfinger snatched a stack of pages, while Mo grabbed the other. Both men began to flip through the pages ravenously.

"Grabbies," Fenoglio chided them. "All these years, and I still remember the characters — the motley folk, the water nymphs, the Black Prince," he wiped his dusty hands on his trousers. "And the villains! The Adder Head, the Fire-Raisers, and worst of all . . . The Shadow! It's a wonderful book, I must say. I'd give anything to go inside myself."

Dustfinger eyed Fenoglio derisively. "Well, get in line, old man."

"I'm missing pages two-twenty to four-eighteen. What do you have?" Mo reached for Dustfinger's pages, but the scarred man held them high.

"You'll do it, right? You'll read me back in?" he said, looking Mo in the face.

"I'll try," Mo agreed. "But not until I get my wife out. And she's safe. I'm sorry but that's the only way I'll do it."

Dustfinger hesitated, but only for a second. He had to tell Mo the truth. "Well, then, we may have a little problem. You can't read her out," he finished quietly.

"What do you mean?" Mo asked, suddenly feeling sick. "Why?"

"Because she's not *in*."

Mo stared at Dustfinger, watching him closely as he got to his feet and left the attic, unable to grasp what he was saying. "What are you saying? Where is she? Where is my wife?"

"I saw her. She's not in the book anymore. She's in Capricorn's village." Dustfinger was walking fast now, heading out the door of Fenoglio's apartment building.

"She's alive?!" Meggie cried as she followed the men and Farid, piecing together what her father and Dustfinger were talking about.

Mo caught up to the fire-eater and grabbed Dustfinger by his collar. He pulled him so close their faces were almost touching. "But we were there! We were right there and you didn't tell me!"

"We needed the book," Dustfinger replied weakly.

"*We* didn't need the book," Mo seethed.

"*I* needed the book," Dustfinger admitted just as Mo threw him to the ground. "What choice did I have?

If you knew the truth, you never would have come here for the book! And without the book you'd never read me back!"

Mo's eyes were full of hatred. "You selfish, weak, repugnant . . . *character*!"

"Blame him — he wrote me that way," Dustfinger said resignedly, motioning in Fenoglio's direction.

"I did," Fenoglio agreed with a shrug.

Mo stared at the scarred man getting up from the ground. What had happened to the "You are not in control of my destiny!" Dustfinger he had glimpsed just hours before? "If Resa's with Capricorn, she's in danger. Tell me how to find her!"

"Not until you promise to read me back in!"

Mo whirled around, his fist raised. Dustfinger protected his face with one of the stacks of pages. "I miss my family, too," he murmured quietly.

Mo lowered his fist and opened his palm to accept the remaining pages. "I promise," he vowed.

Dustfinger slowly lowered the pages into Mo's hand.

CHAPTER TWELVE

ortimer shoved the manuscript pages into his leather satchel. He had to depart immediately.

"I want to help rescue Mom, too. Take me with you," Meggie pleaded, dogging her father's every move.

"You know I can't do that."

"But I can help," Meggie insisted.

"You can help by staying here. By staying safe. That's what you can do." Mo tried to keep calm, but the thought of having more of his family members in peril was just too much.

"You don't know *what* I can do," Meggie replied. Her mind flashed on the talking books in Elinor's library, and her father's amazing reading. "And neither do I," she admitted.

"Meggie — please — not now," Mo pleaded. He understood exactly what she was talking about. It was his worst fear — that she would inherit his . . . gift.

Grabbing Meggie into a hug, he held her close for a moment before pulling away and heading for the door.

Outside, Dustfinger was waiting in Fenoglio's white convertible.

"You! Watch her," Mo commanded the writer, who was standing nearby.

"And Farid as well," Dustfinger added.

"But I want to come along, too! And it *is* my car," Fenoglio pouted.

Ignoring him, Mo gunned the sporty car's engine and took off.

"Bring her back!" Meggie shouted, staring after her dad.

Fenoglio looked from his disappearing car to Mo's daughter and back. "Reduced to babysitting. Marvelous," he griped.

In the station, Elinor waited patiently for the train that would take her home. She could not wait to be rid of this place, but as she looked around she saw families everywhere — parents, children, a grandmother. There were couples, too, and friends. She was the only person by herself, and suddenly she felt a strange pang. She had lived alone for years, but after spending just a few days with Mortimer and Meggie, one thing was clear: She did not want to be alone anymore.

The train chugged noisily into the station and passengers began to board. Elinor did not move.

Mortimer and Dustfinger drove for several hours in angry silence. At last, Mo spoke.

"So if Darius read her out of the book . . ." Mo pictured the unfortunate, disfigured creatures they had been locked up with in Capricorn's stable and tried not to think about the possible deformities Resa could have suffered.

"She's *fine*. Mostly," Dustfinger assured him.

"Mostly?"

"She has no voice. He read her out last spring, and she came out mute. Aside from that, she's fine."

Mo flashed Dustfinger a pained look. Although he was ecstatic that his wife was still alive, he winced when he thought of her without the ability to speak. *Resa is mute*, he thought to himself. The information was difficult to get used to. He let it sink in while Dustfinger listened to Gwin chattering excitedly.

"Pull over," Dustfinger directed.

"For what?"

Dustfinger motioned toward Gwin. The marten was glaring at Mo.

Mo snorted. "Well that makes sense, you speaking weasel." He pulled the car off the road and rolled to a stop.

Dustfinger got out and followed Gwin to the trunk. Popping the latch, he peered in to find Farid curled in a ball, hiding.

"That's one smart rodent," Mo said, impressed.

"But he's mean," Farid complained, begrudgingly climbing out of the trunk.

"Not as mean as Capricorn," Dustfinger cautioned the boy.

"He doesn't scare me. I was raised by murderers and thieves," Farid reminded them.

"Well, he should," Dustfinger said, unswayed and angry at Farid for sneaking into the car. "I should make you walk back."

"I'd only follow you."

Mo chuckled at the defiance in Farid's voice. He looked at Dustfinger, and if he didn't know better, he could have sworn the man was fighting back a smile.

"Get in," Dustfinger ordered.

Farid lit up. "And then after all this, you can teach me Dragon's Breath! Because I've been practicing a bit and —"

Dustfinger cut the boy off and pointed at the back seat. "Just get in the car."

Fenoglio snored in his easy chair while Meggie paced the living room. Though the hour was late, she could not sleep. She could not stop thinking about her father . . . and her mother, and the danger they were in. Suddenly Fenoglio's snores were interrupted by another noise — voices.

"*. . . killed the Wicked Witch of the East?*"

"*I have no brains at all.*"

"*. . . ever since I rusted . . . .*"

Meggie stopped in her tracks and looked around the room, confused. Then she spotted it. Peeking out of her bag was her mother's copy of *The Wonderful Wizard of Oz*!

The voices grew louder, almost as if they were calling to her.

"*You ought to be ashamed of yourself, a big beast like you! You're nothing but a big coward!*"

Picking up the book, Meggie opened it, accidentally releasing a witch's cackle. She stared at the words, which seemed to pulsate. She was ready to try again. . . .

Meggie took the book to an empty room and began to read, quietly. "Dorothy and Uncle Henry could see where the long grass bowed in waves before the coming storm. They heard a long wail of the wind . . ."

Outside, a sudden gale banged the shutters, startling Meggie. "Maybe the cyclone part isn't a good idea," she muttered to herself, thumbing through pages and finding a better spot before trying again.

"It was Toto that made Dorothy laugh. Toto played all day long, and Dorothy played with him, and loved him dearly. He was a little black dog, with long silky hair and small black eyes that twinkled merrily on either side of his funny, wee nose."

The sound of crinkling paper and a tiny yelping bark made Meggie stop again. She looked up to see Toto, the little dog she had just described, sitting on the carpet in front of her looking around in obvious confusion.

For a second Meggie was dumbfounded.

"Toto? Toto, don't be scared . . . you're just not in Kansas anymore," she reassured him.

Toto barked and dashed under the bed.

"*Shh*, you'll get me in trouble! Now come out from under there!" Meggie scolded, anxious to keep the dog from waking Fenoglio.

Too late. There was a knock at the door. Meggie popped up from under the bed in a panic.

"It's me, open the door." Fenoglio's voice was muffled.

"Just a minute," Meggie called. "Not a sound out of you, I mean it," she warned Toto. She pulled the blankets down further on the side of the bed to hide the small dog before opening the door.

Fenoglio smiled weakly when he saw the girl. Basta was right behind him, and before Meggie could scream, the Black Jacket had shoved the writer into the room and stepped in after him. Flatnose followed.

"Sorry, I had no choice. But look, it's *Basta*! And . . . the other one," Fenoglio said, gleeful over the existence of more of his characters.

"Where is your father, princess?" Basta leered.

"I told them he went back, but they wouldn't believe me," Fenoglio shrugged.

"You told them?!"

"He had a knife to my throat! Isn't he *awful*?" Fenoglio chuckled, delighted by his creations.

"Just tell us where Silvertongue is before we kill you *both*!" Basta demanded.

Meggie looked around desperately for an escape, but all she saw was Toto's damp nose sticking out from under the bed.

"You *can't* kill me. You'll *vanish*. That's how it is with writers and their creations. Or don't you know? To kill me is to kill yourselves."

Basta stopped to consider the author's words. His hand moved absently to the good-luck pouch he always wore. Fenoglio smiled. He knew that Basta was ruled by superstitions — that's exactly how he wrote him.

"Yap! Yap! Yap!" All of sudden Toto darted out from under the bed to bark at Basta.

"Toto! No!" Meggie grabbed for the small dog.

"Toto?" Fenoglio looked from the book on the bed to the little dog to Meggie. "My word, she's inherited her father's gift," he marveled.

Meggie cringed. Fenoglio had just blown her secret to the Black Jackets! She hoped, for a moment, they would be too dumb to realize.

But Basta spotted Toto on the book cover. "Another Silvertongue! Capricorn will be so pleased." He grinned wickedly before turning to his men to give orders. "Bring them both!"

Fenoglio's eyes went wide with excitement. Meggie was struck dumb. Only Toto barked in protest as Flatnose grabbed him and dragged him away.

When Elinor arrived at Fenoglio's apartment, it had been ransacked. The floor was littered with furnishings and bedding . . . and Meggie was gone. Elinor felt the wind go out of her. She was too late. Then her eyes fell upon Resa's copy of *The Wonderful Wizard of Oz*. Meggie never would have left that behind, and Elinor knew it. Picking up the charred book, Elinor leaned heavily on the doorjamb. There was only one thing to do.

CHAPTER THIRTEEN

t dawn, Mo pulled the small white car off of the road and parked it behind a cluster of bushes. Cutting the engine he whispered, "We should walk the rest of the way."

Dustfinger nodded and turned to Farid, who was asleep in the backseat with his mouth agape. Dustfinger poked him hard. The boy startled awake and looked around disoriented. Silently, Dustfinger signaled that it was time to go. Farid clambered out of the car. He picked up Dustfinger's bag and followed the men, rubbing sleep from his eyes.

It was still early when they reached the gate surrounding Capricorn's enormous compound. The three slipped past the perimeter wall and up the hillside road toward the village.

Just outside the castle, Mo spied an abandoned burned-out cottage and ducked inside. He needed a little time to formulate a plan. He watched the comings and goings for a long while.

"These guys are just circling the perimeter. We should move in," he said.

Dustfinger pointed to a crude map he had drawn in the dirt while Mo was watching the Black Jackets. "The maid quarters are here. Resa's room is on the ground level, second door on the left if we go in the back."

Mo felt his anger flare. It seemed so unfair that Dustfinger had seen his wife — while he had been missing her so desperately. "*I'll* go in the back. You two can cover me while I'm inside," Mo growled, anxious to be the next person to see Resa.

Dustfinger nodded his assent, then turned to Farid. "Listen to me, this is going to be very dangerous, so you need to stay close. You think you can keep up?"

The boy simply smiled. Moments later Farid was scaling a drainpipe as if he had done it a thousand times before. He scampered noiselessly as a cat onto the roof, and looked around. A few minutes later Mo and Dustfinger hauled themselves up alongside him, red-faced and panting.

"Shall we rest?" Farid asked, looking at their tired faces.

"No, let's keep moving," Mo said, determined.

Farid dashed across the rooftops, a little slower this

time, while Mo and Dustfinger labored to keep up. Soon they were in the alley behind the maid quarters. Mo made his way to the entrance alone.

Slowly Mo opened the back door and peeked inside. The hall stood empty. Creeping as quietly as he could, he passed the first door.

He felt odd, almost nervous, and not because the Black Jackets were swarming the town. No. He was nervous about seeing Resa again. He had been waiting and hoping for this moment for so many years, and he was so close.

Sudden footsteps sped Mo on. In a panic, he grabbed the door handle and ducked inside, pressing his back against the door and listening to his thundering heartbeat.

Mo leaned against the door and listened to the fading footsteps. He was alone in Resa's room. Disappointed that he hadn't found his wife, Mo scoured the small chamber, searching for signs of her — any evidence at all. He saw an apron hanging on a hook, a plain pair of shoes in the corner, and a hairbrush on the bureau. Glancing in the mirror, he spotted something sticking out from under the mattress and hurried over to it.

Lifting the flimsy mattress, Mo pulled out several sketchbooks. He opened the first one to a picture of Meggie as a baby. The likeness was unmistakable, and the evidence was undeniable. Resa really was here. Or at least she had been.

Mo flipped through more pages of the sketch journal. The books were filled with pictures of him and Meggie. Clearly Resa missed them and thought of them as often as they thought of her.

In the last book Mo found images of Inkworld — a journal of the life Resa had been leading without them. Fascinated, Mo paged through, looking at the strange creatures, marketplaces, and landscapes. He felt at once in awe of Resa's experience and a bit jealous that they had not gotten to share it.

In the shadows of the alley, Dustfinger watched anxiously for any sign of Mo. Behind him Farid was puffing furiously, practicing his technique.

"The Dragon's Breath — I think I'm getting close! I feel my ears getting hot! Here! Feel!" Farid grabbed Dustfinger's hand and lifted it to his ear, but Dustfinger brushed him off impatiently.

"It's been too long. I should go check on him."

After looking in all directions, Dustfinger started to step out of the shadows and walk toward the maid quarters.

Without making a noise, Farid yanked him back into a dark alcove. A second later, two Black Jackets passed by so close Dustfinger could smell them.

Dustfinger nodded at Farid, grateful and impressed. Farid beamed back and bowed proudly. As he bent low a bottle slipped from Dustfinger's pack and shattered on the cobblestones with a deafening smash!

Dustfinger glared and Farid looked as if he wanted to die of shame. But neither said a word as they heard the sound of guns being cocked around them. Turning, they saw Cockerell flanked by a number of armed Black Jackets. They were cornered.

"Well, look who's back. And right on time for your execution," Cockerell crowed.

Dustfinger blanched, then lunged at Cockerell only to be hit with the butt of a rifle. Farid looked around, desperate for an escape. He bolted and ran, with a pack of armed Black Jackets hot on his heels.

Inside the maid quarters, Mo was returning the sketchbooks to their hiding place beneath the mattress when he heard an explosion of gunshots, followed by yelling. He ran for the door and quickly made his way out of the building.

Outside, everything was in chaos. Black Jackets shouted to each other as they scrambled to catch Farid, who was racing over rooftops.

Mo watched the boy nimbly dodge Black Jackets, then unexpectedly come back to the spot where he had started. The boy stopped in the alley, breathing heavily.

Mo stepped silently closer. Farid had not seen him, but he could not call to him. He reached out a hand and placed it over Farid's mouth so he would not cry out. He felt the boy start and whip around. His eyes were filled at first with terror, and then relief when he realized it was Mo who had caught him.

After signaling that they should not speak, Mo led Farid down the alley and into an abandoned building.

"What *happened*?" Mo asked when they were safe.

Farid was so overcome with emotion he could barely speak. "They're going to kill Dustfinger. They're going to kill him and it's all my fault," he practically sobbed.

n the edge of the town Cockerell marched Dustfinger toward the castle courtyard. Dustfinger held his head high, though his eyes were downcast as he was forced out of their view.

Cockerell kept up a steady banter as they walked. He spoke as though he had a secret wish to be a tour guide — cheery and full of facts.

"Capricorn's castle is like a fine hotel. We got lots of fancy places to put the likes of you. You'll be kept in the crypt to await your execution. But some of our death row guests get a room with a view."

Before Dustfinger had a chance to infer Cockerell's meaning, somebody grabbed his hair from above and gave it a hard yank. By twisting slightly he managed to get a look at his tormentor. Resa.

The woman swung in a cagelike net over Dustfinger's

head. She glared at her former friend angrily from her hanging prison and gave his hair another hard yank.

If Resa could speak now, Dustfinger knew he would not like hearing what she had to say to him.

"I suppose I deserve that," he conceded.

Dustfinger's Black Jacket escorts burst out laughing to see him taunted by Resa. And under the cover of their noise Dustfinger managed to whisper a few words to her. "Don't hate me. I've told your husband. He's here. We came together. He's come to get you out."

A myriad of emotions played on Resa's face: relief, hope, fear, anticipation, and then pain as a Black Jacket prodded her net, prompting her to release Dustfinger.

To the horrible tune of their laughter, Dustfinger was ushered away without another word.

Trapped in her cage, all Resa could do was watch him go.

Carrying Toto by the scruff of his neck, Basta escorted Meggie and Fenoglio through Capricorn's village. Toto growled, annoyed, and Meggie silently agreed with the small dog. They both wanted to bite the nasty henchman as hard as they could, and would have if they were given half the chance.

Fenoglio did not seem nearly as upset. He acted more like a satisfied tourist as he took in the scenery. As they rounded the corner and Capricorn's castle came into view, the author gawked openly.

"By all the letters of the alphabet, it looks like my book! It's like walking into my own imagination!"

Meggie rolled her eyes, fed up with Fenoglio and his ego. So far his characters had done more harm than good.

On the other side of her, Flatnose leaned closer and whispered to her like a giddy child.

"I wonder what Capricorn will make you read. I hope it's something good. I'm excited, aren't you?"

Excited was not the word Meggie would have chosen. She dreaded finding out which book she would be forced to read. And as it turned out, the real question was which books she *wouldn't* be forced to read.

By the time Huckleberry Finn's raft dropped into the great hall of Capricorn's castle, Meggie had already read from *Cinderella, A Christmas Carol, Mary Poppins,* and several fairy tales. She stood among the gingerbread, glass slipper, and gravestones feeling utterly shamefaced.

"Very well, I'm convinced," Capricorn smirked, happy with Meggie's forced demonstration of her gift. "Though I don't know *what* that boy's going to do without his raft," he mused.

The Black Jackets sniggered at Capricorn's joke — all but Darius, who was standing nearby in his black bowler hat clutching a basket of books.

Still locked in Basta's grip, Toto growled.

Meggie knew just how he felt. "I'm done doing stupid tricks for you. Tell me where my father is," she demanded.

Capricorn shrugged. "I have no idea, and frankly I don't care. You read just as well as he does."

Meggie blanched as she fully comprehended Capricorn's intentions. He planned to keep her as a slave to do his bidding!

Fenoglio, who had been standing silently in a corner watching the proceedings, could not tear his gaze from Capricorn. The expression on his face was a mix of curiosity and satisfaction.

"What are you gawking at?" Capricorn snapped.

Fenoglio answered in a voice filled with wonder. "You are just as I wrote you, 'With a heart as black as ink.'"

Capricorn eyed the old man scornfully, then smiled. "You? Our 'creator and master'? Hilarious," he sneered. He brushed Fenoglio off, disbelieving.

"Shall I prove it to you? Shall I tell you something only a writer would know? Something *not* in the book? Oh, I know! How about . . . your *mother*?"

Meggie saw Capricorn's smile tighten almost imperceptibly. His old maid, Mortola, took a step closer to her master, her eyes flashing.

Fenoglio went on. "*You* say she was of noble birth, and that she died of cholera. But you and I both know she's really just a lowly serving maid. And very much alive." Fenoglio whirled and looked at Mortola. "Isn't that right, Magpie?"

"How dare you!" Mortola shouted.

"You'll pay for your filthy stories!" Capricorn spat. He lunged for the scabbard of a nearby sword, but could not draw it from the stone it was imbedded in. He yanked futilely to retrieve the blade, growing more and more frustrated. "What is wrong with —"

"The girl read it here. Only the king can pull it out, remember?" Cockerell reminded his boss.

A giggle escaped from Meggie's throat. She couldn't help it! Capricorn was evil, but also rather dim.

Abandoning the sword, Capricorn whipped around to glare at Meggie. "Don't you *ever* laugh at me," he threatened. He raised his hand, and Meggie braced herself for the blow.

Toto leaped from Basta's arms and charged Capricorn, barking.

Capricorn recoiled. "Get that dog out of here! You *know* I hate animals! I want it executed with the others!"

"The dog? You want the dog executed?" Flatnose asked in disbelief.

"Take it to the crypt!"

One of the Black Jackets swooped Toto up by the scruff, and Fenoglio hurried to comfort Meggie.

The poor girl felt horrible. It was her fault Toto was here. And now it was her fault that he would be killed.

But Capricorn had not finished. "As for you," he said, turning to Fenoglio, "we'll see how enamored of your creations you are when The Shadow is flaying the skin off your back."

Sweat beaded on Fenoglio's brow. "Listen here, Capricorn — as loathsome as you are, you are no match for The Shadow."

"Besides, you can't bring it out of the book! You burned the last copy! I saw you do it!" Meggie cried.

"Wrong. I kept a copy of the book for myself. Aren't I full of surprises?" Capricorn said, silently congratulating himself on his dastardliness. He snapped his fingers, and in an instant Mortola was beside him holding an ornate box. The lid was sealed with four fists made of steel. After unlocking it, she opened it slowly, and two hissing snakes rose from the inside and wrapped themselves around her arm.

Capricorn reached into the box for the book: *Inkheart*. The very copy that was stolen from Mortimer all those years ago.

"I couldn't burn them *all*, not with my old chum trapped inside," Capricorn said, lovingly opening the book's purple cover. He turned to an illustration of the horrible Shadow and smiled evilly, imagining the devastation the creature could do in this world. "You're going to love him, by the way. And by 'love,' I mean 'cower in terror from.'" With a snap Capricorn shut the book.

Meggie jumped, and Mortola snickered as she returned the last copy of *Inkheart*, and the enchanted snakes, to the box.

"I quite like this world," Capricorn confessed to Meggie, smiling over his own evil plans. ". . . and I intend to write my name on every page of it. You and The Shadow are going to help me do that."

"I won't read anything for you!" Meggie replied fiercely.

"Oh, you think not?" Capricorn smirked.

Standing beside Meggie, Fenoglio finally realized how real the danger was. The pride he felt in his creation changed and he stared at Capricorn with pure loathing.

A short time later, Capricorn himself led Meggie and Fenoglio to the place where they would be held. And, truth be told, he quite enjoyed showing them his conquered village.

"Let me show you what happens to those who disobey me around here," he said lightly as he led Meggie across the courtyard of his castle. He waved his arm, directing Meggie's gaze upward.

Not far off, a blond woman in a red maid's dress swung above them in a net cage.

"She's been very naughty, this one. Tiresome in the extreme. Always trying to escape. Do you feel sorry for her up there? Well you should — that's how you'll end up if you don't read for me."

Meggie stared up through the bindings that held the imprisoned woman. Their eyes met, and a jolt, like an electric shock, coursed through Meggie's body. It had been nine long years, but she would know that face anywhere. She was looking at her own mother!

Resa's eyes, too, grew huge with recognition.

Breaking free of Capricorn, Meggie raced closer and reached up through the binds. Resa kissed her daughter's fingers over and over, hoping Capricorn would not see.

"It's you. It's you," Meggie whispered, hardly daring to believe it. "Don't worry, Mother. Mo is here, too, somewhere. . . . We'll all escape."

Resa looked nervously at Capricorn. He was coming closer with a battery of Black Jackets. She tried to tell Meggie with her eyes that they should keep their bond a secret lest it be used against them. But neither could hide their joy at seeing one another for the first time in years.

"Well, what good fortune! Let me look at you. . . . Ah, yes, I see a resemblance." Capricorn looked from Meggie to Resa and back. His smile grew even more sinister as he stared deep into Meggie's eyes. "Do you still think I can't convince you to read for me?" he leered.

CHAPTER FIFTEEN

s the Black Jackets marched their prisoners through the village to the crypts to await their fates, Meggie scanned the hillside for her father. He had to be there somewhere . . . he was their only hope!

Half in shock, Fenoglio jumped when Flatnose sidled up to him to ask a question. "Is it too late to make changes?" he queried.

Fenoglio squinted at the disfigured man. What "changes" was he talking about?

"I was thinking, maybe if you added a few lines . . . I mean, I don't need to be a great beauty, I'd just like a nice nose, you know?"

"Oh, your nose. Right." Fenoglio stole a glance at Meggie.

"So you can do that? Rewrite a bit? Change things?" Flatnose pestered hopefully.

"I don't know. But it's a wonderful idea," Fenoglio answered honestly. His mind reeled with possibilities of how their situation could be made different . . . .

Flatnose grinned, completely unaware of what he had set in motion.

Descending into the crypts below the church, Meggie slowed. All around them were small chambers filled with coffins.

"Nothing to worry about, child. It's just a bunch of dusty old coffins. If there are spirits down here, we are not the ones they are angry at." Fenoglio did his best to comfort Meggie and smiled to himself when he saw the effect his words had on superstitious Basta, who was busily rubbing his good-luck pouch.

Stopping in front of them, Mortola herself unlocked a chamber and ushered the prisoners in.

Dustfinger peered from between the bars of the next cell. He could not believe his eyes. *"Meggie?"*

"Leave her be! Princess needs to rest that voice of hers for tonight." Mortola shoved Meggie and Fenoglio into a cell and tossed Toto in after them. After locking the cell she headed for the stairs with Basta practically clinging to her skirts.

As soon as they were gone Meggie rushed to the set of bars separating her cell from Dustfinger's. "I've seen my mother — she's a prisoner here."

"I know," Dustfinger said, feeling ashamed.

"Have you seen Mo?" Meggie asked urgently.

Without speaking Dustfinger indicated that Meggie's father had not yet been caught, and they should keep his presence quiet.

Meggie nodded. "Capricorn has a copy of the book. And he's going to make me read The Shadow out of it tonight."

Dustfinger looked at Meggie, wide-eyed.

"I can do it, too," she explained. "I have Mo's gift."

Stunned, Dustfinger let that piece of information sink in and ignite a new hope inside of him. "Then could you read me back?" He had to ask.

Fenoglio answered. "Nobody's going anywhere. If she reads The Shadow out, we're all dead."

Elinor hurtled down the road on a motorbike. It was the first time she had ever ridden a motorbike. It was the first time she had ever attempted to stage a rescue, too.

"This is probably the stupidest thing you've ever done, Elinor," she muttered to herself. "There's an army of murderers up there and you're just a fat old bookworm. You think you can just waltz in there and . . . ."

Elinor trailed off. Her eyes grew wide when she saw what awaited her at the gate. The very same crooked cop that had refused to help her when she was being kidnapped earlier was tied up on the side of the road.

"Well, the shoe's on the other foot now, isn't it, copper?" she grinned.

Inside the crypt, Fenoglio was busy making changes to the manuscript in Dustfinger's pack. He scribbled away on the pages, balling up and tossing aside anything that didn't satisfy him while Toto happily retrieved the paper balls.

At the sound of approaching footsteps, Fenoglio and Meggie quickly hid the pages.

Basta appeared in the corridor, carrying a tray of food. "Food for the little witch. Capricorn wants her to have her strength for tonight," he said, nervously looking over his shoulder as he slid the tray into the cell. The moment his hands were free they flew to the pouch on his neck.

"You should stay," Fenoglio teased the nervous Black Jacket. "We're swapping ghost stories. Oh, that's right, you don't *like* ghost stories."

"I'll give you a ghost story —" Basta threatened.

Then suddenly there was a flash of movement and fur and Gwin was at Basta's throat, busily gnawing something. Basta shrieked and stumbled back, but the marten was gone as quickly as it had appeared.

Basta clutched his throat expecting to see blood, but he was unharmed. For a moment he did not know what had happened. Then he slowly realized . . . Gwin had taken his good-luck pouch!

"You give that back!" Basta shouted at Dustfinger.

"Why don't you come and get it?" Dustfinger taunted him, twirling the pouch by its chewed string. Gwin chattered at Basta from Dustfinger's shoulder, safe in the crypt chamber.

Irate, Basta fumbled for his key, unlocked the door and slammed it behind him. Now he had Dustfinger in a corner.

"What are you doing?" Meggie shrieked, frightened for the fire-eater.

"*Someone* has to get us out of here. That so-called writer obviously isn't gonna do it!"

Fenoglio huffed, taking offense, while Basta circled Dustfinger menacingly.

"Careful, you don't have your luck to protect you now," Dustfinger cautioned.

"Maybe I don't need luck," Basta replied, pulling out his knife.

Putting both of his hands on the coffin in his cell, Dustfinger began to chant. "By the bones of the dead man lying in this tomb, I curse you. May his spirit haunt your every step!"

Basta froze. "Stop that. You take that back!" he shouted. He lunged. Dustfinger sidestepped, and

Basta's blade met only air. "How'd you like me to make both sides of your face match? Time I finished what I started, eh?"

Absently, Dustfinger's hand went to the knife scars on his cheek. Basta lunged again and *BAM!*

From the next cell, Meggie smashed Basta on top of his head with a human femur. Basta wheeled around, stunned and unsteady, to see what hit him. Dustfinger saw his chance. Quickly he grabbed the keys, let himself out, and locked Basta inside.

"You can't run, you know! The Shadow will find you and suck your guts up like a bowl of spaghetti!" Basta threatened angrily. Then he laughed as Dustfinger fumbled to find the correct key for Meggie's cell.

"Only Mortola has that key. She's a very special prisoner, after all."

"Your fire! Use your fire!" Fenoglio suggested.

Drawing in his breath Dustfinger concentrated. His hands glowed. He focused the heat on the lock.

Meggie watched, awed, as the lock began to turn red, like iron on a forge. For a moment she was filled with hope, then the fear returned. Black Jackets were coming. She could hear them on the stairs.

"Help! The prisoners are escaping!" Basta yelled.

The footsteps came faster. Dustfinger turned to flee, to save himself.

"Don't run! You don't have to be the selfish lout I

wrote about, you can be more! You said so yourself! Stay here and save us!" Fenoglio implored, instantly understanding the nature of the character he had created.

Dustfinger paused. He looked for a long second at Meggie. Then he ran, leaving them locked in their cell.

Evading the Black Jackets was easy now — all of their focus was on the crypt and the courtyard. Moving like a cat, Dustfinger soon found himself on a hill on the edge of the village. He stopped for a moment to catch his breath. He looked into the woods . . . and freedom. He was nearly there. All he had to do was keep running. But something stopped him.

Dustfinger looked back at the village. He glanced at the steeple by the courtyard where Resa was trapped and then thought of the crypts where Meggie and Fengolio were being held. The others had all chosen to stay and fight Capricorn, while he, as usual, had thought only of himself.

Behind him Gwin chattered, and after stealing one last look into the woods, Dustfinger made a choice. He took a deep breath and ran, as fast as he could, back toward the village and his friends.

Making his way down the same sidestreets he had just fled, Dustfinger approached the courtyard cautiously. He stepped into a doorway to take cover. Suddenly the door behind him opened and he was yanked inside. His heart pounded as his eyes adjusted to the light. Squinting, he made out the figure before him, smiling. Farid.

"You're alive!" Farid cried.

"For the moment," Dustfinger responded.

Farid threw his arms around Dustfinger's neck, thrilled and relieved to see him still standing. Dustfinger flinched. He never knew what to do with affection. After a moment he gently pushed the boy off. "All right, that's enough."

Mo stepped out of the shadows then, full of questions.

"Did you find them? Where's Resa? And how's Meggie? Where are they?" Mo had watched Meggie being marched to the crypts. He wanted to go after her, but Farid had wisely held him back.

"Everyone's fine, for now. But . . . I . . . Capricorn has a copy of the book. He's had it all along," Dustfinger told Mo.

"What are you talking about?"

"He kept one secretly — that was his plan. To have The Shadow read out of it."

Mo closed his eyes for a moment, shocked by what he was hearing. "That would kill us all. I'm not going to read The Shadow out for anyone."

"That doesn't matter anymore, he doesn't need you. He has Meggie."

"Meggie?"

"She has your gift, Silvertongue."

Mo staggered back with the weight of the news, then sank to the floor. It was the worst piece of information Dustfinger — or anyone — could have given him.

In the amphitheater ruins behind the church, Capricorn surveyed the preparations. Black Jackets scurried about, tending to the last-minute details before the great sacrificing ceremony. Everything was ready. And after the ceremony, the expansion could begin.

"This is a lovely little village," Capricorn said wistfully, staring out at his conquest. "But it'll be nice to have something a bit bigger — stretch out, expand my kingdom's borders." He smiled with satisfaction. Only a whimpering noise, annoying as a mosquito buzzing his ear, interrupted Capricorn's enjoyment of this moment. "Oh do stop whimpering, you're ruining the mood," he complained.

Capricorn shifted the heel of his boot so that it dug more firmly into Basta's fingers as he lay writhing and whining on the ground. "Lucky for you I know the fire-eater will be back for the book. He can't resist it. Otherwise I'd have to make an example of your incompetence and add you to the roster of executions tonight."

At last Capricorn removed his heel. Basta snatched up his crushed hand and staggered to his feet.

Capricorn gave him a look of disgust, then feigned a begrudging smile. "So I suppose just this once I'll have to forgive you. No hard feelings?" He gripped Basta's smashed hand tightly and shook it with mock friendliness, ignoring his underling's cries of pain.

CHAPTER SIXTEEN

ou wanted to be alone so badly, well here you are!" Elinor lectured herself as she crawled through the underbrush close to the village. Her clothes were tattered and her hair had come undone. The differences between reading about an adventure and actually having one were stark, and frankly, a little painful. Instead of sitting home in a wingback chair she was pulling herself through the dirt — sweaty, achy, and muttering to herself like a deranged lunatic.

"Lost in the wilderness. Blisters, mosquitoes. And do you have a plan? No, who needs a plan? I'll just rent a motorbike and buy a map. I'll figure the rest out as I get there. Good thinking, Elinor. Gooood thinking."

Locked in the crypt, Meggie watched Fenoglio with interest. He held several handwritten papers in one hand and a pen in the other. His eyebrows were knit tightly together and he had a pained expression on his face. After scratching out several passages he crumpled up three sheets and tossed them away.

"Having writer's block? Maybe I can help," Meggie suggested gently.

Fenoglio eyed the girl skeptically. "That's right, you want to be a writer someday," he scoffed.

"You say that like it's a bad thing."

"No, my dear," Fenoglio said wistfully. "Just a lonely thing — sometimes the world you create on the page seems so much more alive than the world you really live in . . . ."

". . . and you wish you could be there instead?" Meggie asked.

The writer smiled fondly. She was young, but Meggie was one of the few people he had met that seemed to understand him. "You're a clever girl, Meggie. I could not have hoped for a finer young lady to be stuck in a crypt with while waiting to be executed." He turned back to his pages. "Now — I haven't quite done what *I* need to do yet, but I'm *very* close."

Footsteps echoed in the gloomy passage.

"Oh my, they're very early! Why are they early? This is very inconvenient!" Fenoglio dropped to his knees in a panic and began unballing the early draft pages he had tossed away, searching desperately for something that might work. Toto bounced around, thinking it was a game and confusing matters.

"Stop that now! I'm trying to find something! There was one that was nearly perfect!" He looked at the last rumpled page. "I've found it!"

"Found what?" Mortola stood at the cell door, eyeing her prisoners suspiciously as she unlocked the cell.

"Oh, just a . . . little poem I wrote for the girl. For her to remember me after I'm gone," Fenoglio covered. "Here you are then." He held the paper out to Meggie.

Before Meggie could take it Mortola snatched it away, crumpled it up, and tossed it into a corner.

Toto scampered after it.

"I don't think much of your crude scribblings, old man."

"You are my crude scribblings, Magpie. So I'd be careful of what I crumple up if I were you," Fenoglio retorted.

Mortola glared, then grabbed Meggie by the arm.

"Where are you taking her?" Fenoglio demanded.

"To put on her party dress!" Mortola dragged Meggie out of the cell and slammed the door shut with Fenoglio still inside. "Don't worry, you're invited to the feast as well. In fact, we couldn't eat without you — you're the main course! The Shadow will be feeding on you and that maid later tonight, so rest assured that someone will be back for you later."

Meggie looked back at Fenoglio over her shoulder as she was led away. Their hopes were dashed.

Fenoglio cast his eyes down and saw Toto standing at his feet with the wad of paper still in his mouth, waiting for someone to play.

A few minutes later Meggie was standing on a chair while Mortola tailored the white dress Meggie would wear for the sacrificial ceremony to fit her small frame. Terrified of what was to come, she shook with fear.

"If you don't stop shaking I'm going to stick you with a pin, and I don't mean by accident," Mortola hissed as she tied a black ribbon in Meggie's hair. "You must be very disappointed in your father, Meggie. Imagine, the time you need him most and he's nowhere to be found." She smiled cruelly. "You poor thing . . . abandoned, alone . . . ."

Meggie held back a sob and willed her eyes not to fill with tears. She would not let this awful woman break her!

"Are you going to cry? I hope so. I love to see other people cry. So does Capricorn, actually. He gets that from me . . . ." she said leadingly.

Meggie steeled herself, even as she felt her eyes begin to well, and glared down at Mortola defiantly.

*　　*　　*

In the amphitheater ruins behind Capricorn's castle, rows and rows of Black Jackets waited excitedly in the stands for the spectacle to begin.

Fenoglio squeezed Toto and eyed the crowd worriedly as he was led into the giant cage in the middle of the theater along with Resa.

"Your daughter is a brave girl," Fenoglio told her admiringly.

Resa's eyes widened. This man had news of Meggie!

"If we live through this I'm going to write it all down in a book and Meggie will be the hero," he vowed.

From outside the cage, Flatnose caught Fenoglio's attention. He motioned to his nose as if to say, "Remember what you promised." Fenoglio winked in response, and Flatnose smiled with relief.

Resa was pondering the words "If we live through this" when Meggie was led into the amphitheater. Mother and daughter made instant eye contact, and Meggie raised her chin defiantly. Like mother, like daughter.

Inside the stables, Darius was sitting on a stool reading quietly when a shadow appeared over his shoulder.

"Good evening," said a voice.

Darius nearly fell off the stool as he looked into the face of a dirty, bedraggled, crazy-looking, white-haired woman. "Interested in getting out of here?" she asked.

Unable to speak, Darius nodded.

"Good. Then you're going to have to do a couple of things for me."

Meanwhile, Mo had made his way to the roof of a building that was being renovated. Looking around, he spotted a pile of long wooden planks. Pulling himself out of the hole and moving carefully, he began to inch his way toward it.

In the theater, Capricorn rose to greet his followers.

"Don't try anything funny," he told Meggie as he passed, "or I'll stuff you in a jar. With a reading lamp, of course."

Meggie was silent, but her eyes blazed with anger as Capricorn turned to the audience.

"The time has come to be reunited with our old friend," he said. "For those who have not had the pleasure of meeting him, I promise it will be an introduction you will never forget."

While several men exchanged worried glances, Mortola stepped forward and opened the small wooden casket. The enchanted snakes rose up, hissing wildly. Mortola ignored them and lifted out *Inkheart*, then slammed the lid closed and carried the book to the lecturn.

Meggie's eyes darted about in panic. What was she going to do without Fenoglio's new page? She glanced at the author, who looked as panicked as she felt. Meggie swallowed hard. If anyone knew what The Shadow was capable of, it was Fenoglio.

"Whenever you're ready, cherub," Capricorn said.

Meggie opened the book and stared down at the marked page. Lifting her head, she looked around for her father a final time. There was no sign of him. She had to read. But she never meant for her reading to turn out like this . . . .

"I'm sorry, Mo," she murmured, pushing back her hair.

CHAPTER SEVENTEEN

igh above them, Mo was wrestling with a long plank. If he could just get the other end to rest on the wall of the church across the way, he might be able to cross it. Sweating madly, he reached out as far as he dared and lifted with all his might while the other end of the plank bobbed and wobbled. Finally it plunked into place. He had a bridge to the parapet of the church. A thin, wobbly, anything-but-sturdy bridge . . . but at least it was something.

Mo inched onto the bridge, trying to ignore the fact that he was a hundred feet up. Far below him, Black Jackets patrolled the ground. Mo looked down and was overcome with dizziness. Bad move. Closing his eyes, he took a deep breath. Then he opened them and, looking straight ahead, moved forward.

* * *

Meggie took a breath while her eyes wandered up to the church . . . and spotted her father making his way across the chasm between buildings. Her heart nearly exploded with relief at the sight of him, at the knowledge that he was coming to save them. But he could fall at any second! Suddenly afraid for him, Meggie looked down at the book and began to read.

Shaky and exhausted, Mo finally made it to the church outcropping. Creeping along behind a low wall, he peered down at the ceremony below. He scanned the crowd and saw swarms of Black Jackets guarding entry points, an anxious crowd, Meggie, Fenoglio, and . . . Resa! In a cage! His joy at seeing her alive was ripped apart by the realization that she was trapped like a wild animal. He had to get to her . . . .

"Capricorn led an army of brutal men who struck fear in the hearts and minds of all those he came in contact with," Maggie read, enchanting everyone in the theater with her hypnotic, powerful voice. "But of all the villains lurking in the Wayless Wood, the one most feared and reviled was known simply as . . . The Shadow."

Sensing something, Capricorn glanced up at the

parapet where just a moment before Mo had been looking down on them. There was no one there.

In the cage, Fenoglio pulled a balled-up piece of paper out of his pocket and waved it at Toto, who perked up to play. Fenoglio tossed the paper through the bars and Toto squeezed through to go after it. Grasping the paper in his mouth, he began trotting back to the cage. Fenoglio held his hands up signaling him to stop, then gestured to Meggie. Confused, Toto looked back and forth between Fenoglio and Meggie but did not move in either direction.

"Made from the ashes of Capricorn's victims, The Shadow was immortal and invulnerable, and as pitiless as his master," Maggie read on, her voice growing stronger with every word. She couldn't stop herself from glancing up to the parapet, and caught a glimpse of her father. She hadn't imagined it — he was really here!

Not far away, Toto was weaving through the legs of Black Jackets toward her, carrying the crumbled piece of paper in his mouth.

In the castle, Dustfinger took a sip from a blue bottle and passed it to Farid, who also took a sip. Snapping their fingers in unison, flames appeared in their palms. Dustfinger smiled, impressed with Farid's quick learning.

A moment later a blast of fire erupted from each of their mouths. They walked along the perimeter of the hall, setting fire to everything in sight.

The amphitheater was silent with anticipation as Meggie read on. "He appears only when Capricorn calls him, rising from the ground, a faceless and fiery beast always eager to consume his next victim."

While she read, the earth began to vibrate. The ground smoldered and crumbled and The Shadow rose up . . . a horrific beast of ember and ash.

From up on the parapet, Mo watched, his heart filled with dread. "My God, Meggie. Stop reading. Stop reading!" Scrambling to his feet, he raced down the stairs and into the church.

Far below, Meggie could not hear anything her father said. She kept on.

"Beautiful . . . you're beautiful," Capricorn murmured in awe while others turned away in terror. He swept his arm toward the cage. "Feast, my pet! Feast!"

The massive beast spotted the cage and lowered itself until its burning eyes were level with the trapped prisoners. It opened its horrendous, gaping mouth. Resa and Fenoglio shook with fear.

Meggie stared at The Shadow, frozen with terror and hatred. Her mother was about to be consumed! Just then she felt something tug at her hem. Looking down, she saw Toto drop a crumpled paper at her feet. She snatched it up and spread it flat inside the book on her lap.

A trembling Resa watched The Shadow reach out and touch one of the bars of the cave, causing it to disintegrate instantly.

"Yet one starlit night, The Shadow heard a different voice, the voice of a girl, and when she called his name he remembered; he remembered all those from whose ashes he was made, all the pain, and grief —"

Mortola eyed Toto suspiciously as he made his way back to the cage, and then spotted the page Meggie was reading from. "What is that?" she cried. "What are you reading?"

Fenoglio quickly reached an arm through the bars of the cage and grabbed her hair, holding her back. She screamed in pain.

Enraged, Capricorn had started toward Meggie when The Shadow whipped around and let out an earthquaking roar. Rattled, Capricorn fell.

"The Shadow remembered, and he was determined to take revenge! Revenge on those whose cruelty was the cause of all this misfortune!" Meggie's voice was strong and clear.

"Get the book!" Capricorn bellowed. "Make her stop!"

Fenoglio held tight to Mortola's hair, but she

spun around and bit his hand, hard. "Not my writing hand!" Fenoglio cried in agony.

Resa, meanwhile, was trying to pick the padlock on the cage with Mortola's hairpin.

Mo rushed in, quickly appraising the situation.

"So The Shadow went to his Master and reached out to him with ashen hands . . . ." Meggie directed the fiery monster.

The massive beast did just as Meggie read, turning and reaching silently for Capricorn.

Capricorn's eyes widened in terror. "That's not the book! Those aren't the real words! Someone stop her!" He grabbed a dagger and was about to hurl it toward Meggie when Mo came at him from out of nowhere, pinning his arm.

Mortola's jaw clamped down harder on Fenoglio's hand. Blinded by the pain, he let go of her hair. A moment later she was ripping Fenoglio's newly written page out of Meggie's hand. She held it up, triumphant.

The Shadow instantly pulled away from Capricorn, waiting patiently for its master's next command. "What a pleasant turn of events," Capricorn said, mopping his sweaty brow. He steeled his gaze on Mo and smiled menacingly. "Silvertongue, you're just in time . . . for dinner."

Mo grimaced and tried not to think about being consumed by The Shadow.

Suddenly a bell rang out and everyone turned toward the sound. In the distance, Capricorn's castle was engulfed in flames. Capricorn stared in disbelief. His proudest creation, burning to the ground! "No . . . not the castle!"

The sound of hoof beats echoed in the amphitheater, and Elinor and Darius appeared.

"Attaaaaaaaack!" Elinor shouted.

"Yeah, a-t-t-tack!" Darius echoed.

Behind them thundered the beasts from the stables — the lame Minotaur, the ticking croc, the bent-horned unicorn, and disfigured flying monkeys. Furious at their captors, they raced toward the Black Jackets.

While Meggie, Mo, Resa, and Fenoglio tried to find each other in the chaos, Capricorn watched the scene with amusement. "You think these misfits can conquer me?" he cried, turning toward The Shadow.

"Devour her!" he ordered, pointing directly at Resa.

Mo planted himself in front of the cage. "You'll have to get past me first!" he vowed.

The Shadow came after Mo, darting this way and that as if they were playing a game of chase. Everything The Shadow touched turned to dust . . . .

"Mo, watch out!" Meggie screamed.

Mo dodged The Shadow and watched everything around him burn to nothingness. "Keep reading!" he shouted to his daughter.

"What?!" Meggie shouted back, unable to hear him. "Keep reading!"

"I can't! There's nothing left to read!"

Mo didn't hesitate. "Then write!" He thrust a hand into a pocket and pulled out his wife's fountain pen. A moment later it was sailing through the air toward Meggie.

Meggie caught the pen and looked around frantically for something to write on. There was nothing! She turned to her mother for advice, and Resa signaled that she should write on her skin, her dress . . . anything! Beside her, Fenoglio was nodding encouragement.

The Shadow loomed over Mo. Meggie had to act fast.

Without thinking, Meggie leaned over and began to write. "The Shadow turned away from the innocent!" she read as the pen moved across her arm. "And back to the evil master who had controlled him all these years . . ."

The Shadow pulled away from Mo and turned its attention to Capricorn.

". . . The Shadow reached for him with ashen hands and, and as it did, Capricorn began to crackle and fade like the old page of a book."

Capricorn's eyes began to grow pale and crackled, like parchment.

Her arm full of words, Meggie moved onto her legs. ". . . growing transparent and thin as paper . . . ."

"I won't let you!" Capricorn screamed out, grabbing a hold of Mo's leg in a death vice. Mo struggled, but could not break Capricorn's grip. And a moment later Mo's face began to turn to paper, too.

"Dad!" Meggie screamed.

"Keep reading, Meggie!" Mo told her.

Meggie watched her father struggle to stay in this world. "I can't!" she cried.

"Save your mother. Read, Meggie. Read!"

"Don't leave me!" she cried.

"I'll never leave you, Meggie! Read!"

Capricorn held tight to Mo until — *THUD!* — he was hit in the side of the head with the padlock from the cage.

"Leave him be!" Mortola screamed protectively. "That's my son!"

"Yeah, well, *that's my mother*!" Meggie screamed triumphantly.

Mo, out of Capricorn's grip, regained his color almost instantly. He locked eyes with his wife, smiling into her face.

"Capricorn's ink-black soul filled with terror as he saw the end was near . . ."

Mortola ran for her son, but Basta, who was being attacked by Toto, backed into her just as a flying monkey pulled down a huge tapestry and threw it over them, trapping them underneath.

"And so, too, did the souls of all those within The Shadow's gaze who had committed villainy in Capricorn's name! And then they blew away — like ashes in the wind."

Mo looked up and saw Capricorn go pale, his features flattening and crackling like old paper. A shadow passed over him, and he screamed, collapsing into a figure of dust and ash that scattered in the night breeze. All around the amphitheater, Black Jackets turned to dust, while the villagers screamed and ran. Within moments the theater was virtually deserted.

The Shadow looked around and let out a mournful roar.

"And in an instant, all those who had been summoned against their wills were set free, and set right, and sent back from whence they came."

Fenoglio stared at Meggie as he listened to her words, knowing at once that she was a powerful person, a powerful reader.

"Please . . . set *me* free," he asked quietly.

Meggie looked into the writer's face and understood. "And the old creator finally got his wish, disappearing into the world he had only dreamed about."

Fenoglio waved good-bye to Mo, then disappeared. . . .

"... while the terrible monster himself disintegrated and was no more."

The Shadow looked around, horrified by his own fate, then fell to his knees. A moment later there was an explosion of shadow and ash ... and he was gone. And one by one the deformed creatures, the Minotaur, the homely maids, Toto, and everyone who had been read into this world were pulled back into their own books, their own lives.

"... And then finally, after what was almost a lifetime of wishing, the young girl's most heartfelt dream came true as the mother she always knew she'd see again and the father she cherished ..."

Meggie stopped writing and looked up at her parents, her eyes filled with tears.

"... came running to embrace their only ..."

Meggie was enveloped in the arms of her parents. She buried her face in her mother's arms.

"Meggie ... Mo," Resa said, using her newly found voice.

The family stared in amazement at each other, their eyes filled with tears, then they embraced again.

"Oh, stop now," Elinor complained. "It's unseemly to cry at happy endings."

Mo reached out an arm and pulled Elinor into the group hug.

CHAPTER EIGHTEEN

ust outside the theater, Dustfinger watched the happy scene with an ache in his heart. Behind him, Farid came running from the castle.

"What happened?" he asked breathlessly. "I missed it. They're all gone." He was quiet for a moment, then added, "He'll never read me back now."

"What are you talking about?" Farid asked. "He said he'd try after he got his wife back."

"He won't. He'd never risk losing her again. And I wouldn't make him."

Confused, Farid turned away from Dustfinger and gazed at the scene in the amphitheater. Everyone was talking and laughing, happy. Farid turned back to Dustfinger, relieved. But Dustfinger was gone.

"Dustfinger?" Farid called. There was no answer.

*   *   *

Elinor beamed at her niece. "Well, Mortimer has a great deal of repairs to do on my books of course, but Meggie kept your seat in the library warm for you," she told Resa.

"She let you in the library?" Resa replied, shocked. "I had to sneak in when I was a girl."

"Oh you did not," Elinor objected. "You talk as if I were some kind of prison matron!"

Resa and Meggie exchanged a knowing glance. That sounded about right!

Suddenly Mo sensed something behind him. Turning, he spotted Mortola and Basta crawling out from the heavy banner that had been thrown over them.

Meggie's eyes widened. "Mo, what are they —"

"I don't know," Mo cut her off.

They watched in disbelief as Mortola hobbled to a pile of ash — the place where Capricorn had died — and sank to her knees, weeping.

"What have you done to my boy?" she wailed.

In an instant, Mo and Basta locked eyes on a discarded rifle that lay on the ground between them. They scrambled for it, and Basta snatched it up. Resa, Elinor, and Meggie gasped.

"Witches, sorcerers," Basta shouted.

"Take it easy," Mo soothed.

"Stop talking! Your words are like poison! Look what you've done!"

Mortola looked up from her son's ashes, her eyes red from crying.

"We have to get out of here before one of them starts reading again," Basta cautioned.

Mortola glared at Basta with hatred, but knew he was right. Together they backed out of the amphitheater, Basta's rifle fixed on Mo and his family.

"Not how books are supposed to end, is it? Well guess what? From here on you're living in a horror story. So lock your doors," Basta snarled.

"Stop him!" Darius yelled.

But no one dared move.

And then they were gone, disappearing into the night.

"Terrific," Elinor said grimly. "That'll give me nightmares for weeks."

Mo leaned over and read Meggie's arm. "Those within The Shadow's gaze . . ." he read thoughtfully. "They were under that tapestry. The Shadow couldn't see them."

A fiery explosion rocketed toward the sky, and they all turned to see Capricorn's burning castle. It was almost beautiful, like an otherworldly fireworks display.

"Let's get out of here," Mo said, taking his wife's hand. Just as their fingers entwined he saw a figure dash by. He eyed the lectern. But it was empty.

"What is it?" Meggie asked.

"The book," Mo said slowly. "The book is gone."

Outside the village, Dustfinger stood on a bridge that crossed a huge chasm. He stared into the darkness below. Deep in thought, he barely noticed Gwin eying him curiously.

And then another figure was there, too.

"You were going to leave without me?" Farid asked.

"You'd be better off with the others," Dustfinger replied absently.

"Well, if you're going, you should probably bring this with you." Farid said as he held out a copy of *Inkheart*.

Dustfinger stared at the book. "Where did you get that?" he asked.

"I stole it. Who knows how the story ends?"

Dustfinger took the book and began to walk away when suddenly he heard the sound of footsteps pounding behind him.

"Dustfinger! Wait!" cried a voice. Dustfinger turned. It was Mo.

"I promised," said Mo, heaving for breath. "It's your turn now." Mo extended his hand out to Dustfinger, and as their eyes met, Dustfinger understood. Mo was going to read him back into the book, back to Inkworld.

Dustfinger's mouth stretched into a slow smile. "Thank you . . ." he said breathlessly. But just then Mo remembered something terrible: Fenoglio had said that Dustfinger dies at the end of the book.

"A-are you sure?" Mo asked him. "You remember what happens at the end . . ."

But nothing was going to keep Dustfinger from getting home. "It's like I said," Dustfinger shrugged, "my fate is in my own hands now."

Dustfinger smiled, and Mo took it as his cue to open the book and begin to read. "It had been many years since Dustfinger had set eyes on the wheat fields and the old windmill," he began, "but it was even more beautiful than he had remembered it . . ."

Suddenly Dustfinger found himself free-falling through the sky. He landed with a thud as his body made contact with the hard earth. He looked around in amazement. It had worked! He was home!

Inkworld was exactly as he remembered it: the shimmering fields of wheat, the rolling hills, the windmill that sat high on a hill, and there — at the top of the hill — a woman in red. *Is it her?* thought Dustfinger, hardly able to contain his emotion. He picked himself up off the ground and ran toward the woman. He was finally home!

*   *   *

Back on the bridge, Meggie and Resa spotted Mo and Farid in the distance and jogged over to where they stood. The two men were looking around in confusion. Dustfinger had disappeared! And in his place was a beautiful multicolored hummingbird. The tiny bird flitted playfully around their heads before diving deep into the gorge beneath them.

Mo watched the bird descend out of sight as he said with disbelief, "He's gone back."

"Back where he wants to be," said Farid, looking down at the ground sadly.

"Well, what about you?" asked Mo.

"I can't follow him," Farid explained as he rummaged around in the bag Dustfinger had left behind. "But I've kept Gwin behind," he said, holding the furry little creature up triumphantly, "so the end of his story will be different. He's not going to die after all!"

Mo, Resa, and Meggie all exchanged quizzical looks.

"But what will you —" began Mo.

"— he can stay with us!" exclaimed Meggie quickly.

Mo gave her a questioning look.

"It was Mom's idea!" she said in defense, as Resa glared in her direction. "Just don't expect me to read you back," she joked to Farid.

The four exchanged looks and exploded into laughter.

It was the first bit of joy Farid had felt in a long time. He grinned. He was happy — and most importantly, he finally felt like he belonged.

Mo, Meggie, and Resa sat together on a grassy hillside watching the sun rise. Mo pulled something out of his pocket, and it gleamed in the early morning light.

"I believe you dropped this," he told Resa, slipping her wedding ring on her finger and leaning in for a kiss.

"You have to tell us what it was like in Inkworld," Meggie insisted. "I want to hear every last detail."

"It wasn't all terrible, you know. Some of it was beautiful," Resa replied. "But you go first. Tell me about your first day of kindergarten, and how you learned to ride a bike. Tell me what you want to be when you grow up!"

Meggie looked at Mo questioningly. Did he still object to her choice?

"She wants to be something very dangerous," Mo said gravely.

"Oh?" Resa asked, her face registering concern.

"A writer," Meggie said.

Mo smiled. "She's going to be a good one, too." He looked at his cherished wife and daughter, then at the blazing remains of Capricorn's castle. The flames darted and danced against the sky, momentarily shaping themselves into things from other worlds — a bear, horse . . . possibly even Dustfinger. The fireblower's figure jumped for joy, then faded into the darkened sky. Yes, Meggie would be a wonderful writer — he was sure of it.